A MARRIAGE MOST SCANDALOUS

SCANDALOUS BALLROOM ENCOUNTERS BOOK 2

VICTORIA VALE

CHAPTER 1

BRIGHTON, 1816

Sheridan Cranfield stood in the doorway of his wife's dressing room, peering through the half-open door into her chamber. She sat at her vanity alone, facing the mirror, her honey-blonde tresses hanging down to her waist like a curtain of spun gold. A yellow dressing gown had been cinched at her waist, undoubtedly covering one of her prim, white nightgowns. She held a lock of hair over her shoulder and brushed it with rhythmic strokes, her eyes unfocused as she stared off into the distance.

He wondered what her thoughts consisted of, if she anticipated him coming to her with the same eagerness he felt.

Steady, Sheridan, he chastised himself. *You don't want to frighten her.*

The madness of his lust for her had become a tangible thing—one that had been driving him insane. Yet, his wife remained an innocent, newly initiated to the marriage bed.

This reminder did not douse the fire in his loins as he stood there, watching her perform the simple task like a voyeur taking in a tawdry exhibition. Sometimes, he liked to run his fingers through her silky locks, marveling in the erotic caress of them against his skin. But then, that just led to imagining giving it a rough yank, pulling her head back to expose the column of her throat before plundering that exposed, vulnerable skin with his mouth.

He shuddered at the thought and his erection throbbed, becoming downright painful. Not a night passed when he did not toss and turn in his bed, suffering from dreams of the forbidden fantasies he wished to experience with his lawful wife.

However, he could never touch her that way, sully her like he would a brothel whore. She was his wife, and thus, deserved his utmost respect and gentle care. A young woman, she'd just finished her first Season when they'd met in Bath.

In those days, he still suffered from a broken heart after having been rejected by Margaret Seymour. Though, he must remember to think of her as the Duchess of Avonleah now. She'd spurned him for another man, claiming to love him. He'd retreated just before the end of the Season and avoided attending their wedding, hoping to nurse his wounds in the serene environment of Bath while taking the waters for his health.

There, he'd found Cecily Montgomery and fallen so utterly in love that Margaret's rejection became a distant memory he hardly recalled. She'd charmed him with her pretty smiles, dazzling him with her beauty. Yet, as he'd come to know her, he'd found her to be smart, witty, and kind. Her compassion awed him, most of all. A member of various ladies' charitable societies, she spent much of her free time tending to orphans, feeding the poor, and helping others in any way she could.

The daughter of an Earl, she'd been raised in the lap of luxury, her every whim catered to. Her large dowry had hardly been needed. While Sheridan had yet to inherit his father's title of Viscount of Perth, wise investment and management of his allowance had expanded his own wealth tremendously. As such, he was happy to allow her complete access to her dowry to use as she pleased, though she seldom indulged beyond the occasional gown or hat.

Three months of marriage, and she had made him delirious from happiness. Aside from the fact that his crude fantasies were likely to drive him insane. Try as he might, he could not rid himself of them.

His father's teachings came back to him now, reminding him of why he could never indulge, no matter how much he might want to.

A gentleman's wife is to be treated gently, as women possess delicate constitutions. A man must ensure that he is never aggressive in his amorous attention, lest he frighten or traumatize her unduly. Copulating with one's wife is for the sole purpose of producing an heir, a duty to be taken seriously by both parties. With his mistress, a gentleman need not practice such restraint. Not gently bred, courtesans and whores can endure all manner of treatment, since they possess hardy constitutions and the knowledge of how to fulfill a man's baser needs.

Along with his father's words came the distasteful memories of the 'lessons' accompanying them, causing him to shudder. The viscount had ensured that his own beliefs concerning marriage and sex had been so deeply ingrained in Sheridan that they could never be undone.

Despite knowing it would be socially acceptable for him to take a mistress, he could not bring himself to do it, no matter how burning his urges. When his day ended, he wanted nothing more than to come home to his wife. No mistress could bring him the warmth and companionship she did.

Bad enough he bothered her more than he should to ask for his marital rights. Yet, he couldn't stay away. It did not help matters that she welcomed him with kindness and an eagerness to please him. He wondered what she would think of him if she ever knew it would gratify him to treat her like a common tart.

She would be disgusted with you.

Sucking in a deep breath, he turned away from the door, crossing toward the washstand. He must calm his racing blood before he went to her, lest he be tempted to sweep the contents of her vanity table to the floor before bending her over it, lifting her dressing gown to reveal her perfect, round arse, and fucking her in a mindless fit of passion.

No, he must never do anything so crass. He was a gentleman and she, his lady … he would get a grip on his wild fantasies before going to her bed.

Closing his eyes, he opened his belted dressing gown. He imagined her undressing him, parting the robe to find him naked underneath, her fingernails raking the light blond hairs sprinkled over his chest and in a thin line down his abdomen. He gritted his teeth and took hold of his hard cock, stroking it once firmly. His knees buckled and his stomach clenched, pleasure washing over him as he imagined pushing her to her knees before him, fisting her hair, and thrusting into her open mouth. Her plump lips would feel so good around him, her tongue hot and wet.

A man visits a whore if he wants someone to suck his cock, not his wife.

Grunting in frustration, he shoved the unwelcome thought aside and tried to regain hold of his torrid fantasy. Thinking about it wouldn't be so bad, would it?

He conjured up the sight of her naked breasts, large and rosy-tipped. His throat went dry as he imagined laying her down and fitting his cock in the valley between them, his fingers caressing the nipples while he pressed them together and thrust back and forth. Her tits must be the most marvelous pair he'd ever seen, soft and round and his to touch and taste. Ah, how he wished to fuck the cleft between them.

His hand tightened around his member, his strokes growing faster and less refined. In less than a minute, he spent, snatching a cloth from beside the washstand to catch his seed. His chest heaved as he fought to control his breathing.

He hardly felt satisfied, but better prepared to join his wife without fear that he would send her running from him in a fit of tears. The closeness and intimacy she offered him would have to be enough to satisfy.

If he could not live with that, then perhaps he could find a new home in Bedlam.

Cecily stood when the door between her dressing room and bedchamber swung open. She smiled, turning to greet him, hands folded before her. As always, the sight of him caused her pulse to race. She had married a beautiful man. He stood tall and slender, his tousled, golden hair shadowing spring-green eyes as he approached her. His features appeared refined, if even a bit ethereal. With the glow of the lamplight cast over him, he almost resembled some heavenly being.

And he was hers.

Unlike most marriages of the *ton's* lords and ladies, theirs had been a love match, something she'd never thought to hope for when striking out to find a husband. Sheridan had spent the entire season courting a lady who'd gone on to marry someone else. Fortunate for her that she had; otherwise, he'd have never come to Bath, where she'd accompanied her arthritic aunt who'd wished to take the waters for her ailments.

She'd ended the season without incurring an offer, a happenstance which had caused her to feel a bit maudlin at the time. When he'd asked her to dance a minuet with him during a fête at Bath's Upper Assembly Rooms, she'd been swept away, captured by his gallantry and charm.

From that evening on, they'd been inseparable—strolling along the Royal Crescent to take in its scenic architecture and sprawling, green parks; meeting for breakfast chaperoned by her aunt at a little coffee-shop that had fast become a favorite haunt of theirs; browsing the circulating libraries for tomes to pore over together.

They'd spent lazy afternoons in the park, seated on one of the benches as she read to him from their chosen book, or window-shopping on Milsom Street. She'd come to love him for more than his easy charm and good looks. Within the four weeks they'd spent together in Bath, she'd come to love Sheridan Cranfield for the man he was.

To cap their whirlwind romance, they'd conducted a simple ceremony at Bath Abbey, with the few acquaintances they knew who'd sojourned to Bath after the season in attendance.

After their wedding, he'd whisked her away to Brighton for a honeymoon, where his family owned a residence facing the sea on Marine Parade. From their bedroom, a balcony stretched out toward the beach, offering them a lovely view of sunrises and sunsets.

They bathed in the ocean, walked along the sand, picnicked on the grounds of the house, attended balls and card assemblies at the Castle Inn and the Old Ship, and the theater in New Road. Her wedding trip proved to be a marvelous time, filled with romance and companionship with her husband.

Spring fast approached, which meant the time had come to return to London. The season would begin and when Parliament sessions resumed, Sheridan would again take up his seat in the House of Lords.

Life would be as it had been; only now, she would be married to the man of her dreams.

There remained just one problem.

As a lover, her husband left much to be desired.

It wasn't that she found their coupling unpleasant. Their first mating had been painful, but his tenderness had caused it to fade quickly, and by the end, she'd come to appreciate the closeness she'd experienced while having him inside of her. Yet, there seemed to be so much missing from the experience. At least, for her.

Her mother had been very frank in explaining marital relations to her, so she'd found nothing surprising or unexpected about the experience. She knew where all the various body parts were supposed to go, and that it resulted in the creation of children. Her mother had warned her that it wasn't always pleasant and some men could be selfish, not at all interested in pleasing their wives.

If she did not know her husband so well, she might believe him to be selfish, when their every coupling ended in satisfaction for him, and the opposite for her. However, she'd come to realize that lack of care on his part was not the problem. Nor lack of desire. She saw his hunger for her every time their eyes met, and when his stare raked over her from head to toe. Sheridan loved her; she believed that. He also desired her.

Unfortunately, he lacked finesse when it came to making love, a fact she'd long resigned herself to. Her mother had always told her the marriage bed existed for the purpose of bearing heirs for one's husband. She should not have expected to gain her own pleasure from it. Yet, every now and then, he would touch her or kiss her in a way that left her yearning ... and she knew there had to be more. The promise his caress gave her proved something else existed beyond the monotony of their lovemaking.

Still, she remained uncertain of how to broach the subject with him—or even if she should mention it at all. She did not want to hurt his feelings or make him feel inadequate.

So, she became determined to make the best of it and focus on the things she did enjoy ... like when he held her close and kissed her as he did right now.

"Did you enjoy the theater tonight, my love?" he asked, tilting her chin up and smiling down at her.

The radiance of that smile stole her breath away and she found her heart squeezing in her chest.

"I did," she replied, resting her palms on his chest. The heat of him became apparent through the fabric of his dressing gown. He was slender but wiry, with corded muscles stretched beneath supple skin. "I have so enjoyed our time in Brighton. While I am anxious to return to my charity work, I will miss the seaside and our seclusion here. I don't want to have to share you with the *ton*."

He chuckled, causing his chest to rumble beneath her fingers.

"I am loath to leave it behind, too. Yet, our duties call us back. But never fear; I am always yours when you wish me to be. There is no duty that can distract me from ensuring you are kept happy."

"Just now, I am delirious with happiness," she replied, rising up on tiptoe to kiss him once more.

She parted her lips, a soft sigh emitting from her throat as the taste of him lingered on her tongue. His grip on her waist tightened, the evidence of his arousal swelling between them.

"Shall we adjourn to the bed, darling?" he murmured, his lips still against hers, his hands already loosening the belt of her dressing gown.

"Yes," she whispered, allowing him to remove the robe.

His hands came up to the buttons of her nightgown and he loosened them one by one, slowly revealing a deep vee of bare skin from her neck to her navel. He gasped, his breath catching and holding as his fingertips grazed the valley between her breasts. A curvy woman, she had always been self-conscious about her body—her large breasts, most of all, which earned her salacious gazes when she wore her more daring gowns. But her husband's gaze on her bare chest made her feel beautiful, womanly. As he pushed the gown from her shoulders, his eyes locking onto her nipples, she felt like a goddess.

"So beautiful," he murmured, gently palming one breast. "You're so lovely, Cecily."

She whimpered and closed her eyes. This was the part she liked best—when he touched her with his beautiful, long-fingered hands.

"Sherry," she murmured, his nickname. He liked it when she called him that.

His fingers stroked her nipple, causing it to stiffen and pucker. His breath felt warm on her skin when he lowered his head to taste it, his tongue swirling around the hard peak. She panted, arching her back and offering herself to him. His hands moved, skimming her breasts, fingers walking along her ribs, then taking hold of her waist.

His grasp on her ribcage tightened more, his hands shaking as if he held himself in check. He often trembled this way when they made love, as if just touching her overwhelmed him. The thought alone sent shivers down her spine. To know a man could experience such desire for her made her feel empowered.

His tongue on her breasts caused small flutters between her thighs as she grew wet. She wanted him … oh, how she wanted him. But not the timid, reserved man carrying her to the bed now and laying her on the sheets like he handled a piece of priceless china.

No, she wanted the passion she knew he could give her if only he would cease holding back from her. His very touch and kiss seemed calculated, like he'd planned his lovemaking in advance and refused to deviate from their usual routine.

When he entered her, electricity crackled over her skin, causing her to crave more. His low moans in her ear made her more desperate for more. She arched her back and opened her thighs wider, hoping it would be invitation enough for him to quicken his pace, to do *something* other than slowly enter and withdraw until he spent in a hot rush of liquid.

She held him close when it ended, running her fingers through his sweat-dampened hair. A smile crossed her face when he mumbled that he loved her before drifting off to sleep.

"I love you, too," she whispered, pressing her lips to his forehead. "With all of my heart."

Their love would be enough. Not only were they espoused, they'd become friends who enjoyed each other's company. She knew ladies who hated their husbands and even lived separate lives from them. She felt fortunate to have found someone to love. Surely, she couldn't allow something as insignificant as sex to ruin what they had.

He loved her. It had to be enough.

CHAPTER 2

$\mathcal{W}$hen Cecily and Sheridan arrived in London, they settled into their rented townhouse in Grosvenor Square. His father, the viscount, would have gladly allowed them to stay in one of the many rooms of Perth House, the family residence in town. However, Sheridan had told her he did not wish for their honeymoon period to end.

"I want you all to myself, my love," he'd said when she'd asked him why they'd rented their own, smaller house in the same neighborhood as Perth House. "How can we be alone with my parents and brother underfoot?"

She suspected there must be something he would not tell her—some other reason he wished to avoid the company of his father. She'd only met the viscount once, but had sensed an undercurrent of tension between them. The same resentment seemed to emanate from Sheridan's younger brother, Aaron. When she'd asked him about it, he'd told her that it was nothing, and she shouldn't worry.

She'd refrained from asking him about it again.

Now that they'd arrived in London, they had obligations to fulfill, friends to call upon, and soirées to attend. The second morning after their arrival, she paid a morning call to her best friend, Penelope Hunt, stepdaughter of the Marquis of Hartford.

"Cecily, *darling*!" Penelope exclaimed as she was shown into the drawing room. "How good it is to see you. I vow, London has been so dreadfully dull without you. Though, I suppose I can hardly begrudge your husband the honor of your company."

Cecily swept forward and wrapped her arms around Penelope. "Oh, you cannot know how happy I am. Being married is simply ... oh, it has just been wonderful!"

Her friend smiled and ushered her toward a loveseat before which a silver tea service and Wedgewood china had been placed. She rang for the butler, ordered a plate of biscuits, then turned to face Cecily once they were alone.

"You and Mr. Cranfield have been the talk of the town since your wedding in Bath. Everyone, oh absolutely *everyone*, has hailed your match as the romance of the season!"

"I do not know if I'd go so far as to call it that," she demurred.

"Oh, but it is," Penelope insisted as the biscuits were delivered. She poured tea for them both and laced Cecily's with sugar and milk— exactly the way she liked it. "And just think, if Margaret Seymour had not tossed him over, he might never have found you in Bath. Ah, but such is the beauty of Fate, is it not?"

"I believe it is Margaret Rycroft now. Her Grace, the duchess of Avonleah."

"Quite a surprise, that match," Penelope remarked with raised eyebrows. "Perhaps even more so than you and Mr. Cranfield. Tell me, darling, is he good to you?"

She sighed, feeling a smile tugging at the corners of her mouth. "He is perfect, Penelope. I know you are of the opinion that there is no such thing, but Sherry is simply ... he loves me, you know."

"I do not doubt that he does, my dear. I do hope this happy phase of your marriage lasts."

Her friend's comment should not have surprised her. Approaching her third season without nabbing a husband, Penelope had become a bit jaded. There had been a romance during her first season that had ended bitterly, though her friend never liked to speak of it. The man had broken her heart and she'd hardened herself, convinced no man would be worth having.

To become a spinster seemed her aim, and in a few more years, Penelope would be firmly—and quite happily—on the shelf.

Despite her knowledge of this, Cecily's smile faded as she lowered her teacup into the saucer. "Whatever do you mean?"

Penelope shrugged. "I do not mean to alarm you, darling, but Mr. Cranfield is a man like any other. They all have their vices. Men of the *ton* are known to be slaves to those vices, and that includes their whores and mistresses."

Her mouth fell open at her friend's crass language.

"Good heavens," she gasped.

"I so hate to infringe upon your happiness, dear, but surely, your father kept a mistress?"

Her mind raced as she tried to remember any details from her adolescence that might shed some light on that particular mystery. If her father had kept a mistress, he must have been the most discreet man in all of London. She'd had no inkling.

"I do not know," she replied. "But surely, not *all* of them keep mistresses."

Penelope shrugged again, taking a bite of her biscuit. "Those who can afford them do. Those who can't ... well, there are always the brothels for them."

Shock rippled through her, turning her stomach. She'd never known her friend to be so worldly about such things.

"Sheridan would never ..." She lowered her gaze and swallowed past the lump in her throat. "He loves me."

Penelope set her hand upon her knee, a sympathetic smile upon her face.

"I do not doubt that he does," she murmured, "but men have carnal appetites they do not fulfill with their wives. Wives bear children and manage the home. Mistresses and whores please them sexually. It does not mean they do not love us."

"Us?" she snapped. "You have never even been married."

Instead of being insulted, Penelope laughed. "No, thank heavens, but my mother has … twice. My father—God rest his soul—kept a mistress, and, I do believe the Marquis still keeps a bit of skirt here in town."

Cecily saw an opening and changed the subject to the events of the upcoming season and the latest fashions for the remainder of their visit. However, her mind could hardly get invested in the conversation.

Could Penelope have been right? Now that their honeymoon had ended and they had returned to town for the season, would Sheridan keep a mistress? Would he visit her, and make love to her, and perhaps even … oh, it was too hard to think of. She'd heard of men who bore bastard children with their mistresses. Just the thought of him siring a child on another woman made her ill.

By the time the visit ended and she set about her short walk home, she'd come to a decision. Her marriage would never come to that—secrets kept about mistresses and illegitimate children. She remained confident in Sheridan's love, and her ability to please him.

Did she please him? While the marriage bed had left her feeling a bit unfulfilled, her husband always seemed happy when they finished. Even if they made love almost exactly the same way every time. Even if there existed no variety, and very little passion.

But what if Penelope had the right of it? If a man had deeper urges than the ones he fulfilled with his wife, then where would he go to satisfy them? Sherry certainly had made no such demands on her, even though she would have been ecstatic if he had. She often had wicked thoughts … thoughts she knew no gently bred lady ought to have. Yet, she'd been afraid that to tell Sheridan her secret desires would cause him to grow disgusted with her. He'd married a lady, not a whore.

And yet … if she could fulfill his needs, he would have no need for mistresses or whores.

Brow furrowed in concentration, she walked on, determination causing the wheels in her head to spin rapidly.

Sheridan hadn't been in London for all of two days before his bosom beaus came looking for him. They hadn't all been able to attend his hasty ceremony in Bath, and so insisted that a proper celebration was to be had—men only—complete with drinks, women, and debauchery.

While he'd insisted that he shouldn't, they'd insisted otherwise. They'd even gone so far as to call on him at home and enlist Cecily's aid in convincing him that a gentleman's evening would be just the thing to celebrate their new marriage.

His wife, of course, being an innocent lady with no knowledge of such evenings and all they entailed, had encouraged him to go and enjoy himself.

"We've been in each other's pockets since the wedding," she'd said with one of her sweet smiles. "That old adage about absence making the heart grow fonder is quite true, my love. Go, and enjoy the evening with your friends. I shall be quite content to spend the evening at home."

"Very well," he'd relented. "But only if you and I spend the entire afternoon together tomorrow. We can do whatever you like."

She'd given him a sly grin and declared she'd like to go shopping on Bond Street, where he was to walk beside her in silence and tote her purchases. He'd agreed, and after allowing his valet to dress him for the night, he'd joined three of his best friends from university in the coach that would carry them to Brooks' for cards and drinks. He heard talk of visiting a brothel, but rather hoped they'd become so involved in their card game that all mention of such debauchery would be forgotten.

No such luck.

"Now that the honeymoon is over, have you grown quite bored, Sherry?" asked Tristan Coburn.

The redheaded second son of an earl sat to his left, eyes focused on his cards with a cigar clenched between two teeth.

Sheridan's gaze flitted from his hand for a moment and he frowned. "Bored? Why the devil would you ask such a question?"

His reply came out a bit terser than he'd meant it to be, but weeks of holding back while making love to his wife had him on edge. The slight fulfillment he found in the marriage bed did very little to squelch the raging fire that had taken residence in his veins.

"Oh, come now," urged Bartholomew, Tristan's elder brother and heir to the earldom. "I have been married for five years now, Sherry, so I know better than these numbskulls. You must be quite ready for a bit of fun."

He took a long swallow of brandy.

"I'll thank you to mind your own business, both of you," he snapped as the liquor burned a path through him. He was slightly inebriated, and well on his way to being quite foxed. "Cecily and I happen to enjoy each other's company. In fact, I'm rather unsure of why I chose to spend the evening with you rather than her at the moment."

John Barrett, third son of a baron and naval officer home from sea for a short time, nudged Bartholomew and chuckled. "See how agitated he's become? He's positively bursting at the seams. Something must be done."

"Quite right, old chap," Tristan slurred between gulps of brandy. "A visit to Madame Petra's is in order, before he snaps and kills us all."

"A possibility that becomes more likely by the second," Sheridan seethed from between clenched teeth.

"I say, Sherry," Bartholomew added, "do calm down. No one disputes that you love Mrs. Cranfield. Who wouldn't feel affection for such a lovely, amiable woman? You can hardly be faulted for giving in to your baser urges. That's the way of the male species."

"She never has to know if you're discreet," Tristan piped up. "A mistress tucked away out of sight is just the thing."

"I don't want a mistress." He'd started growling now, a knot of anger working its way through his chest.

"Quite so," agreed Bartholomew. "A quality mistress could set a man back several thousand pounds, whereas a whore can get the job done just as well for less money and no fear of her becoming overly attached."

Sheridan's fingers tightened around the decanter of brandy they shared as he poured himself another snifter. He wanted to stand and dash his glass against the wall and rail at them that he did *not* need sexual release at the hands of a whore or mistress. He desired his wife; he *loved* her.

Yet, he became acutely aware of the fact that he hadn't slept for days, his body wound taut as a crossbow. Perhaps they—and his father —were right. If he spared Cecily the baser needs of his sexual urges, she'd likely thank him for it. The fantasies that would reduce her to nothing more than a tart ... well, they'd be better enacted on a tart, wouldn't they?

Guilt seemed an unnecessary emotion. He was a man, and this was the sort of thing he'd been raised believing to be proper.

Then, why did he feel nauseous at just the thought of touching someone who wasn't Cecily?

By the time he'd finished his drink, he'd resolved himself not to do it—to cry off and go home after the brandy ran out and they all grew tired of cards.

But then came the drink after that, and then he really became quite foxed and unable to think past the pulsating vein filling his cock with blood and reminding him of his unfulfilled urges. Which just caused him to drink more. When at last he stumbled from Brooks' flanked by three equally foxed, randy men, he'd quite forgotten that he'd decided accompanying them to a brothel would be a terrible idea.

It wasn't until they stood in the parlor of the famous Madame Petra's bordello that he remembered.

He should never have come here.

However, the Madame had come into the vestibule to take their coats and greet them, and it really would have been quite rude of him to leave now. Of all the brothels in London, Madame Petra's had been hailed as the best. It boasted the softest beds in the most opulent settings, the cleanest, most beautiful women, and a Madame who was the consummate hostess.

Not to mention ravishingly beautiful.

To call her pretty would have been an injustice to the lady. Indeed, she appeared quite fair of face, but he could think of many ladies of the *ton* who possessed equal attractiveness. There existed *something* about the woman—a sort of decadence and inherent sensuality no man could resist. She remained well-known among the men of London for the girls she hand-selected to work in her brothel, in addition to services provided behind the closed doors of the city's most elite residences.

Sheridan did not know specifically what services she provided, but rumors of men who hired her to lay with both them and their wives abounded, along with other scintillating whispers he'd never paid much attention to. As he stood in the vestibule, inclining his head to her in greeting, he thought of her in his massive four-poster bed, a writhing, moaning Cecily between them. A fresh surge of blood filled his cock. He bit his lower lip to suppress a groan and tried not to stare.

It had become bloody hard not to. She stood tall, with endless legs showcased by the high-waisted gown clinging to her every curve. A lithe and lean figure, with breasts that would fill a man's palms and hips that would, as well. Her skin glowed an exotic, olive shade, and her dark, sable hair had been cut in a short, fashionable style to frame her face in loose waves. She wore light cosmetics—rouge stained her lips red, and kohl made her brown eyes even more dark and fathomless.

"Gentlemen," she purred in a deep, lightly-accented voice.

No one quite knew where the Madame came from, but tales of her background varied. She was Italian—no, Greek—no, half English, half Egyptian. Her father had been a merchant—no, an exotic sultan—no, a duke who had borne her illegitimately with a foreign princess. Whatever the case, that accent of hers only added to her appeal.

"Welcome. I am Madame Petra. What's your pleasure this evening?"

Sheridan kept his eyes on the Persian rug beneath his feet while his friends placed their orders. Tristan and John liked to share, redheads their favorites. Madame Petra knew just the girl, and placed them in the care of a maid who would take them to her.

Bartholomew was greedy, and never shared. In fact, he often overindulged, the reason why the Madame had sent him off with a second maid to a pleasure room where three whores would await his delight. Shooting him a devilish grin, his friend left him standing there in the hall, with only the Madame for company.

She studied him in silence for a long time before speaking. "You do not wish to be here, do you?"

Her soft, low tone surprised him. He started, glancing up at her with undoubtedly bloodshot eyes.

"I beg your pardon?" he slurred.

She took his hand and lifted it, eyeing his wedding band. "You are a newlywed. Your ring shows no sign of age and you have the dazed look of a disillusioned husband about you."

He glowered at the Madame. She proved too perceptive by half, and her nearness set him on edge. The only woman he ever had such a visceral attraction to was Cecily. It must have been the brandy, he decided, and the sensual atmosphere of the brothel.

"What business is it of yours?" he snapped, snatching his hand away.

Instead of responding with irritation, she folded her hands before her and kept her cool eyes fixated on him.

"It is my duty to ensure that the men who patronize this establishment leave happy. What can I do to make you happy, Lord ...?"

"Cranfield," he supplied. "And I am not disillusioned. I love my wife."

She inclined her head and pursed her inviting lips. "I can see that you do. Your friends cajoled you into coming here because they can see you are sexually deprived. You need stimulation that your wife does not provide."

His hand shot out to grasp her arm in a bruising grip. She flinched, and if he wasn't mistaken, shivered a bit in his hold.

"I will not stand here and talk about my *wife* with a *whore*."

Despite his insult, she lifted her chin and fixed him with a haughty stare.

"I go by 'Madame,' if you please, my lord, not 'whore.' And we do not need to talk. I can see quite clearly what you need. Follow me."

She turned and began to walk, with his hand still wrapped around her arm, forcing him to let go as she sashayed toward a darkened corridor.

"Where are you taking me?" he asked, his voice coming out a bit gruff. He hated that this woman inspired such lust in him when his beautiful wife waited for him at home. He hated the fact that no matter how wrong he knew it was, he wanted so very badly to go wherever she led him.

She turned and smirked at him, her eyes dancing with amusement. "There is a way you can enjoy yourself here without being unfaithful to your wife. Don't you wish to know what that is?"

Curiosity, it had been said, killed the cat. And so, too, was he led toward absolute destruction by his own inquisitiveness.

Where they went, he soon discovered, was a darkened hallway. The narrow corridor lay shrouded in blackness so thick, he had to hold his hands out and feel his way along. He could hear her breathing and the swish of her skirts as she preceded him.

"Here we are," she murmured, her voice no more than a whisper.

He halted, his every muscle tensing when he brushed against her.

The soft swell of her bottom fell against his crotch, the friction causing a primal reaction. He bit back a groan and fought the urge to lift her skirts and bend her over right there in the dark hall. A sliver of light appeared, slicing through the darkness. It shone on Petra's face when she turned toward him, the dark eyes assessing.

"If a man cannot touch, he is always free to watch," she purred. The light increased as she swung open a door and preceded him inside. "Follow me."

He obeyed, and found himself in a small but opulent chamber decorated in sensual shades of red. The plush carpet beneath his feet, oversized furniture, and the scent of jasmine served to further enhance the comfortable, downright sexual feel of the room.

She turned to face him, hands clasped behind her back. Candlelight caused her dark hair to gleam and brought out golden flecks in her irises.

"Sit there, if you please," she murmured, motioning toward a large, plush armchair just behind him.

Eyeing her warily, he backed into the chair and sat.

She crossed the room, took hold of a sheer, red curtain, and pulled. She moved from one end of the room to the other, using the curtain to block his view beyond it. The candlelight glowing on the other side cast a few shadows against the gossamer fabric.

She turned and gave him a glance over her shoulder. "Enjoy yourself, my lord."

CHAPTER 3

ONE HOUR EARLIER ...

Cecily studied her surroundings with wide-eyed curiosity. The room she'd been ushered into appeared as opulent as any in a Grosvenor Square townhouse; yet, she remained aware that she stood in a house of sin. *A brothel.* Her parents would suffer an apoplexy to know it.

Yet, she resolved to succeed in her quest for sexual fulfillment within her marriage. After leaving Penelope's house that afternoon, she'd contemplated the best way to go about it. She couldn't very well sit Sheridan down and tell him she'd been displeased with his performance in bed. Besides, she doubted she could ever find the words to properly express how, even though she went unfulfilled, she still loved him.

Thus, her plan to accost him at Madame Petra's bordello. When his friends had come to invite him out for a gentleman's evening, she'd been thrilled. She might have been an innocent maid at the end of last season, but she knew this sort of evening typically ended with the men adjourning to a house of sin. If what Penelope had told her proved true, Sheridan would be looking to ease his urges at a place like this. If she knew her husband, Madame Petra's would be his establishment of choice. The first son of a viscount would be accustomed to the best of everything, and that included whores.

Whore. The word sent a little thrill down her spine when she met her own gaze in the gilt mirror. Reflected behind her was the decidedly sensual bedchamber with its massive, mahogany four-poster bed dressed with black curtains and red tassels. The silk robe she wore concealed the scandalous attire she'd been given. The deep, wine color of the material enhanced her coloring—bringing out the golden hue of her hair, deepening the tone of her blue eyes, and calling attention to her smooth, alabaster skin. She wore cosmetics for the first time, and found she liked their effect. Dark kohl enhanced her eyes, and rouge invited attention to her lips.

Observing her appearance, she thought absently of the woman who'd aided in her transformation. She'd only come prepared to speak with the Madame and perhaps enlist her aid concerning Sheridan. A few months ago, she'd never have thought someone like her existed, or that she'd ever have need of her services. Yet, here she stood, several thousand pounds poorer. However, the Madame had come highly recommended. If she couldn't help them, no one could.

She hadn't expected for Petra to be so warm and kind.

The Madame had ushered her into a private sitting room, where she'd promptly rung for a pot of chocolate and a tray of assorted cakes. In the plush, comfortable surroundings of the room done up in shades of black and gold, Cecily had felt instantly at ease. When Petra had urged her to tell her the problem, she'd told her everything—her and Sheridan's whirlwind courtship and hasty marriage, as well as the troubles they'd experienced in the bedchamber.

"I love my husband, Petra," she'd said, fingers wrapped tight around a mug of steaming chocolate. "I just want ..."

The Madame had moved from her chair across from her and settled onto the loveseat by her side. They'd sat so close, their thighs had brushed, and Cecily had felt the first fluttering of attraction for another woman. It had both frightened and excited her as she'd gazed up from her cup to find the Madame scrutinizing her with dark, fathomless eyes.

"You want passion," Petra had murmured, reaching out to pat Cecily's knee.

It was madness to wish the woman would trail that hand higher, caressing her thigh. Yet, Cecily had found herself wishing for it fervently. What was happening? Attraction to another female was something she'd never experienced before. What would her husband think of such a thing?

"Yes," she'd whispered, trembling as Petra took her cup and set it aside.

The Madame had taken one of Cecily's hands in both of hers. "There is nothing wrong with that," she insisted. "Nor is there anything wrong with you for wanting those things. Women are passionate creatures, despite the quiet, dowdy mice men try to make of us. We simply have to show your husband the truth."

She'd bit her lower lip nervously. "Could *I* be a passionate woman? I have never had the chance to discover whether or not I could be."

With a soft smile, Petra had released her hand and reached toward her. Cecily had stiffened and gasped, but hadn't pulled away as Petra began removing the pins holding her hair securely at the nape of her neck. Lock by lock, her hair fell loose, tumbling down her back. Petra had stroked the strands, her eyes seeming to soak in every detail of Cecily's appearance. The fact that Petra was so beautiful should have intimidated her. Yet, she'd become acutely aware of the fact that the Madame's gaze became appreciative the longer she gazed upon her. She'd liked what she saw.

Once her hair fell loose, the Madame had stroked it, trailing her fingertips through the strands, then lower over the column of her throat. Cecily's pulse had raced as her heart thundered in her chest. She'd been taken by surprise when Petra had leaned toward her and swiftly covered Cecily's mouth with her own. Her muffled gasp had melted into a sigh as soft, feminine lips had molded to her own.

Cecily had returned the kiss, never doubting her actions for a moment. Petra's mouth had felt light and sweet, so natural, against her own. It had made her feel bold and desirable ... wanton. Petra had traced the side of her face with one fingertip, then caressed lower, hooking the digit in the neckline of her gown. Cecily had shuddered when the fingertip had brushed one nipple, causing it to blossom and harden.

Pulling away, Petra had given her a cat-like smile and licked her lips.

"I think you're doing yourself a disservice," she replied. "You're already a far more passionate creature than you, or your husband, even realize."

The door to Cecily's right opened, jarring her from the memory, and she turned to find Madame Petra. Her face heated as she remembered their shared kiss.

"Are you ready?" the woman asked, her lightly accented voice a soft purr in the candlelit room.

Cecily turned to face her, fingers fumbling with the knotted belt of her robe. "I hope so. Do you think he will come? Perhaps I've misjudged him."

The Madame gave her a little half-smile—just the slightest curve of her plump lips. "He will come, and when he does, you will be ready for him."

She gave herself another cursory inspection in the mirror. "I do hope he will enjoy it. I'd hate to think that he will be angry or disgusted with me."

The Madame stepped forward and took one of Cecily's hands in hers. "You love your husband, don't you?"

"More than anything."

"Your willingness to do everything to please him has made that evident. Do not worry, sweet Cecily. We will give your husband a show he is not likely to forget. Then, we will help him to unlock the animal in him just waiting to be freed."

She shivered again, her nipples going hard against the silk of the robe as the image of an animalistic Sheridan tearing her clothes from her body and ravaging her played through her mind.

She could hardly wait.

"Remain here," Petra said, releasing her hand and turning to leave. "I will return once he is in place. And stop worrying. You look beautiful, and he will be pleased."

She then found herself alone again, with nothing left to do but wait. The seconds seemed to crawl by, and as they accumulated to minutes, she fought anxiety. The risk she'd decided to take could result in the fulfillment of her wildest fantasies … or it could cause her to lose the man she loved. Nothing left to do now but hope the first result would come true. There could be no other outcome.

The things the Madame had instructed her to do—to allow Petra to do to her—had caused an embarrassing blush to heat her face. Yet, they also intrigued. Oh, she must be a wicked creature if such things could tempt her body and mind. If her husband found her wickedness pleasing, then she had nothing to be worried about.

If not … no, she would not think of that now.

She didn't know how much time had passed, but by the time Petra returned, it felt as if she'd been waiting for hours.

The Madame's eyes glittered with excitement. "He is here," she whispered. "Are you ready?"

Her heart began to pound, and she feared the thrumming of her pulse would choke off her air supply. She could not respond with words, so she nodded.

"He is just through this door."

Before she could think, Petra had taken her by the hand, leading her through said door. They entered a chamber similar to the one they'd just left, decorated in the same sensual hues. Cecily's held breath released on a sigh of relief as she noticed the sheer, red curtain cutting the room in half. The shadow of a man seated in a chair fell against the fabric, dark and mysterious.

Sheridan.

She took a shaky breath and closed her eyes, fighting to remain calm. She did this for him—for them.

Petra grasped her shoulders, causing her to open her eyes. The woman stood close, so near their bodies almost touched. The hands on her shoulders felt soft, gentle but firm. Her fingers stroked over the silk-covered shoulders, and her breath caressed Cecily's cheek. She pulled her, leading her closer to the curtain, until their silhouettes appeared against the fabric.

"Close your eyes," she whispered. "He cannot see your face yet, and I won't let him until the right moment. Enjoy yourself, Cecily. I intend to."

She obeyed, allowing her eyelids to fall and her breath to escape her lungs in a slow exhale. She stiffened when the other woman's hands came to the knotted belt, but forced herself to relax as it loosened. The silk fell away from her body, teasing her skin as it went. Heat rose in her cheeks when she was revealed to the gaze of the other woman, wearing far less clothing than she ever had in front of another person other than her husband. The lingerie she had on was nothing a respectable lady would ever own, making them perfect for this clandestine encounter.

A black corset cinched her waist, accentuating the flare of her hips and thrusting her full breasts upward. A pair of black stockings covered her legs to mid-thigh, tied with vibrant, scarlet bows. Her only other clothing consisted of a pair of black mules. She wore nothing else—not even a pair of drawers. Her hair fell past her shoulders in loose waves.

She felt Petra's fingers stroking her locks, trailing down her shoulder. A fingertip traced her collarbone, then the valley between her breasts. Her hand found one of the exposed globes and squeezed. Cecily gasped, excited by the little tremor that the palm caused against her nipple.

Disappointment stabbed her when the hand fell away, but when she opened her eyes, she saw where that hand had gone. Petra had started undressing, loosening the fastenings of her gown down the back. The front of the garment sagged, then fell away. In a whisper of satin, it pooled at her feet. She wore nothing beneath it.

Cecily's eyes widened and shock parted her lips. The woman proved even more beautiful nude than fully clothed. Envy stabbed low in her belly. She'd always been 'pretty', but this woman embodied all that sensuality entailed. Sex and passion in human form. Long limbs framing a sinewy body ripe with curves, her olive skin offset by the triangle of dark curls covering her mons. Dark brown nipples, large and round, drew the eye.

She snuck a peek at the curtain, finding their shadows perfectly outlined there. So similar, yet so different—one long and sinewy, the other round and lush with curves. She could hear Sheridan's breath hitching on the other side of the curtain, feel his eyes on them through the fabric.

Petra reached for her, pulling until their bodies rested flush against each other. Another soft sigh escaped her lips at the feel of the other woman's soft curves against hers. Their nipples brushed and hers hardened even more, becoming painfully taut. Petra's hand cupped the back of her head and she lowered hers until their lips met. The other woman's tongue caressed the seam of her lips and she parted them, meeting it with her own.

Petra moaned, wiggling against her and causing the most intriguing friction. She reacted instinctively, wrapping her arms around the other woman, allowing her fingers to sink into soft, pliant flesh.

If what Petra had told her about the tastes of men proved true, the picture they made would stir Sheridan. Hell, she grew aroused by the sight of Petra's olive skin against her porcelain, the feel of the woman's soft thighs against her own, their breasts touching, their nipples brushing.

She could never have imagined another woman could provoke her lust her so.

Petra's hands cupped her breasts and lifted them, kneading softly at first, then with increasing pressure. Cecily moaned, arching her back, offering them up at a better angle. She grew wet between her legs, and an insistent throbbing began deep inside.

"You have beautiful tits," Petra murmured, lowering her head to taste one. "So soft and lush."

Her mouth was warm, her tongue gentle and slow as it circled one pink nipple. The dark beauty ran her tongue from one breast to the other, lapping them, nipping at them with her teeth, teasing them with soft, slow sucks. The cries of pleasure echoing from the ceiling were wild, increasing in pitch as the suckling pulls of the mouth around her nipple caused an answering throb between her thighs.

Behind the curtain, she registered movement and the rustle of fabric, Sheridan's ragged breathing and low murmur of appreciation for what he witnessed. She closed her eyes and imagined him freeing his cock from his breeches and stroking it with a strong, firm hand. She'd seen him do it once, when he hadn't realized that she'd walked into his dressing room. After watching for a few moments, she'd left the room, desire causing her cunt to ache so badly that she'd yanked up her skirts and pleasured herself to the image burned on the back of her mind. It hadn't taken her long to figure out that stroking the little button buried within her intimate flesh, what was called the clitoris, could bring her satisfaction. She'd longed to feel her husband's hands there.

Moisture seeped from her core, soaking the soft thatch between her thighs. She brought her hands up to Petra's head, her fingers threading through strands of thick, wavy hair. She tilted Petra's head back, lowering her own for a taste of her tits. The feel of the other woman's tongue on her breast had left her curious as to how a feminine nipple would feel in her mouth, how it would taste.

Petra gave a low purr, arching her back and reaching down to cup Cecily's buttocks. Their mounds touched, downy blonde curls caressing dark ones. Petra rotated her hips, grinding against her and groaning low in her throat as Cecily's tongue strokes grew bolder.

"Bloody hell," Sheridan rasped from the other side of the curtain, his voice dripping with arousal and heavy with breathlessness.

The nipple in her mouth drew away, and Petra knelt in front of her, her mysterious gaze burning into Cecily's. A smirk curved the corner of her lush mouth as her fingers delved into the damp curls covering Cecily's mons. She gasped when slender fingers slid between the lower lips, encountering the velvety folds.

"My friend here is so wet, my lord," Petra called out, so that Sheridan could hear from his side of the curtain. She leaned forward and parted Cecily's curls, exposing her swollen clitoris. Swirling her tongue around the little bud, she made a low sound, as if tasting something heavenly. The heat and friction of her tongue caused Cecily's knees to buckle. "Mmm, she tastes even better than she feels."

Sheridan didn't speak, but his sharp intake of breath gave voice to his state of arousal.

Petra licked her again, running her tongue from Cecily's opening, up over the sensitive pink folds, circling around the throbbing, hidden bud. Another moan tore from Cecily's throat, and her hips moved toward Petra, a silent plea for more. No one had ever told her such an intimate thing was possible. It felt better than anything she'd ever experienced. She wanted to feel Sheridan's searching mouth there, his hot tongue going where Petra's had been and beyond.

"Would you fancy a taste, my lord?" Petra asked, as if having read her mind.

She could practically hear his indecision the pause in his breathing, the break in the sound of his hand stroking his own cock.

"No," he said.

Yet, his voice held a note of uncertainty, a huskiness that belied his refusal.

"Pity," Petra murmured. Her breath tickled Cecily's sensitive mound, sending a tremor down her spine. One of her fingers probed inside, invading her slick sheath. "So tight, too, my lord. Tight as a virgin. So sweet. You don't know what you're missing."

He grunted in frustration. "I can't."

"Of course you can," Petra replied, her finger continuing to wreak havoc on her insides. "My friend wants a man's touch ... *your* touch. Don't you, my love?"

"Yes," she rasped, her voice sounding foreign to her own ears. It came out deeper, throatier, a purr of desire.

Petra stood, breaking contact. Cecily bit back a groan of disappointment. The game they played had come to a crucial point. Time to move on to the next phase of it, and if Petra had been right, it would prove even more exciting than the first.

CHAPTER 4

On the other side of the curtain, Sheridan wrestled with indecision. Through the sheer veil, he could see two silhouettes and just enough detail to make out what they did to each other. In the back of his mind, he knew this must be wrong. He should have gone home to his wife. Instead, he found himself drunk, trapped in a room with two panting, groaning females, and a cock that had gone hard as stone. No amount of stroking with his own hand could tame it now. It had taken on a life of its own, craving the wetness and heat of a woman's cunt.

Cecily's cunt.

But if he went home now, he would surely stumble into her room and fuck her in a mindless fit of drunken lust, likely frightening her to death in the process. His need had grown to a level of ravenousness that defied all reason. He craved something—anything—to squelch it. His wife never had to know. In fact, she'd probably be grateful that her animal of a husband had slaked his lust elsewhere.

"There is a blindfold beneath your chair, my lord," said the Madame's deep, smoky voice. "Put it on."

Brandy had weakened his will, and his cock had taken over the thinking for him. He obeyed her. The black fabric darkened his vision, heightening his other senses. The curtain whispered open and soft footsteps padded across the carpet toward him. A pair of hands came down on his shoulders, caressing downward toward his chest. His cravat fell away and cool air whispered across his skin as his shirt came apart, button by button.

"You are so tense, my lord," Petra murmured.

Those must be her hands touching him, the slender fingers undressing him.

"Let my friend take care of you. You may pretend she is your wife, if that is what you need. She can be anything you wish her to be."

The scent of feminine arousal clogged the air around him, causing a fresh surge of blood to his cock. A pair of feminine legs straddled his and the weight of a second person came down on his lap. He bit back a string of curses as a woman's thighs met his and a hot, weeping pussy came to rest against his cock. The woman sighed softly, moving her hips so that her wet folds glided over his shaft, soaking him in her juices. She was so damned wet, just as Petra had said.

"Fuck," he growled, his chest heaving with the effort it took to hold himself in check.

"Yes, my lord," Petra whispered with a throaty laugh. "Fuck her. She is ready for you."

He clenched his jaw, fighting the urge to thrust upward into the inviting little sheath teasing him with its nearness and wetness.

"I was promised a taste," he said.

The scent of this woman had intoxicated him. His mouth watered to have that sweet cunt in his mouth.

"You heard him," Petra said, her voice a gentle command. "If it's a taste he wants, then you will give him one."

Silently, the woman in his lap stood. Her fingers stroked his hair, tilting his head back. The touch caused his scalp to tingle. The scent of her arousal grew stronger, and her leg came up over his shoulder, coming to rest over the back of the chair.

Sheridan opened his mouth and his palate became flooded with the taste of woman. He groaned, suckling hungrily, letting his tongue roam at will over the wet, silky flesh. The woman moaned, one hand gripping his shoulder for balance. Her curls tickled his lips, soft and downy. Her scent and taste invaded his senses, sweet and floral.

He brought his hands up to her hips, allowing his fingertips to sink into the soft flesh of her buttocks. She felt buxom, with hips that overflowed in his hands. It seemed easy to pretend this woman and Cecily were the same, when they possessed similar body types. He urged her to ride his tongue, coaxing movement from her hips while he lapped and sucked like a starving man. She shuddered, following his lead and rotating her hips in tandem with his tongue strokes. Her moans rose to screams, and he recognized the signs of a woman close to completion. He increased his efforts, latching onto her clit and drawing on it mercilessly.

One of his hands moved back between her cheeks, then delved forward, finding her opening. He thrust two fingers into her, pushing another cry from her lips. He imagined Cecily straddling his face, her cheeks flushed with passion as she rode him to her climax.

His cock pulsed, and he nearly came then and there. Instead, he intensified the pressure of his tongue and increased the rhythm of his strokes inside of the tight little sheath gripping his fingers.

The woman splintered, crying out one last time and trembling against him. Her channel tightened around him, pulsing and contracting. She went limp against him, sinking back down into his lap.

But Sheridan wasn't finished with her yet. He lowered his head, searching for breasts he knew would match the hips in ampleness. His open mouth caressed a collarbone, and the soft curve of one shoulder, then made its way lower. When the tight bud of one nipple brushed his lips, he opened and consumed it. A soft whimper became his reward, and the woman's hands tangled in his hair again, pulling, caressing, encouraging him to take his fill.

"Ah, Cecily, you taste so good," he murmured. Behind the darkness of the blindfold, he imagined it was her he touched in the way he'd always wanted to, unrestrained and without fear that she wouldn't like it.

"Get on your hands and knees," he grunted, deciding he couldn't take anymore. He needed release, and he needed it now. "I want to fuck you from behind."

Her weight left his lap, and he stood. "Madame, I know you're still in here."

"I am, my lord," came Petra's voice from somewhere behind him.

"A sheath, if you please," he said curtly. If we was going to fuck someone other than his wife, he'd be damned if he sired a bastard on her.

"Right away, my lord."

He went to his knees on the carpet, reaching out and finding the woman right where she should be—in front of him and on her knees, her arse lifted and tilted upward in invitation. A few seconds later, Petra's hands found his waist, then slid forward, gripping his cock. He hissed, thrusting into her hand. She gave him a light stroke, then sheathed him with the condom. After tying it off, she reached down and gave his bollocks a little squeeze. Sheridan cried out, his gut contracting in response to the bold caress.

Then, she was gone again, retreating silently, leaving him alone with his mystery woman.

Sheridan wasted no time. Taking her hips in his hands, he pulled her back onto his erection. She gasped, and he let out the breath he'd been holding. Her cunt gripped him tightly, creating the friction he craved as he pulled out and slammed into her again.

She screamed when his pelvis pounded against her buttocks, causing the soft flesh to quiver in his hands. He repeated the motion again and again, slamming into her with brute force that surprised even him. Gritting his teeth, he rode her mercilessly, undoubtedly leaving fingerprints in her flesh as he held her at the angle he desired. She didn't seem to mind his rough treatment. In fact, the harder he pounded her, the louder she cried, until her hips swayed back against him, urging him on harder and faster.

"Cecily," he groaned, thrusting even faster and harder, causing his bollocks to slap against her mons. "Christ, you feel so good."

"Sheridan," she whimpered, swaying back into him one last time and quivering in release.

In the back of his mind, he latched onto the sound of his name falling from this whore's lips. For that moment, he conjured Cecily's voice. It seemed so vivid. It almost felt real, as if she were truly present.

With one last groan, he fell against her, his release causing his stomach to clench and his lungs to burn with the effort it took to breathe. He sucked in a ragged breath, trying to calm his racing pulse.

After a moment, he pulled away, sinking back onto his heels and resting his hands on his thighs. He heard movement in the room, and realized he didn't want to lose the secrecy of anonymity. He didn't want to have to look at the woman he'd just had sex with and shatter the mystery and illusion. It seemed easier not to face what he'd done now that it was over. But Petra's hands were on the back of the blindfold, and soon, it would all end.

"Wait," he said, too late.

He closed his eyes, almost tempted to keep them closed. He could feel their gazes on him, two pairs—Petra's and the whore he'd fucked in a mindless stupor.

"It's all right," a voice called out to him. Sweet, gentle, soft. All too familiar. "Look at me, Sherry."

His eyes flew open, and a fist of anxiety rose up in his throat. Trying to swallow past it, he grasped for something to say—anything —but no words came forth.

The blue eyes boring into his appeared full of compassion and tenderness, and … and something else. Satisfaction?

It had been her the whole time. He could hardly believe what he saw. Had he wished for this so fervently that he'd conjured her doppelganger?

There could be no other explanation for this.

Or, it really was her. His wife. Here, in a whorehouse.

When he forced his tongue to come unglued from the roof of his mouth, he could only manage one word in a hoarse, ragged whisper.

"Cecily?"

CHAPTER 5

ecily paced, her eyes watching the progress of her bare feet over the soft carpet. Hands clasped tight before her, she worried her gold wedding band between two fingers. Pausing, she craned her neck, hoping to catch hold of some sound that would tell her Sheridan had arrived home. Breath held, she dared not even swallow lest she miss the open and closing of the front door, or the sound of his footsteps on the stairs.

After the blindfold had been removed to reveal her, his expression had been nothing short of flabbergasted. He'd gaped, eyes wide and mouth ajar for a full minute before he recovered. He'd glanced from her to Petra, who stood nearby, still nude. She hadn't missed the spark of attraction between the Madame and her husband, or the resentment that followed when he realized he'd been tricked. Then, perhaps, had been a bit of relief. She'd known he hadn't wanted to sleep with a whore—or what he thought to be a whore. He hadn't wanted to dishonor their vows; that much had been obvious.

She could certainly understand the combination of confusion, guilt, relief, and satisfaction he must have been feeling in that moment.

"It's all right," she'd said, reaching out to cup his face. "I planned the whole thing. I wanted to surprise you."

"Well," he'd said, his Adam's apple bobbing as he paused to swallow. "You have certainly succeeded."

He'd stood, refastening his breeches.

Cecily had followed his lead, accepting the dressing gown Petra extended to her. She'd pulled it on and tied the belt.

"Well? Won't you say something?"

He'd given her a blank stare, his expression betraying nothing. "Did you hire a hack to bring you here?"

She'd blinked, taken aback. "Yes."

"Did you tell it to wait?"

She'd nodded.

"Good. Go home."

Her fingers had found the sleeve of his shirt. "Won't you come with me?"

"My companions will wonder what's become of me. Under no circumstances can I allow them to know you've been here. I will return home shortly."

He'd been right, of course. She would leave as discreetly as she'd arrived, and when he came home, they would speak of what had happened. She could only hope he'd understand why she'd acted as she had.

'Shortly', as it turned out, proved far longer than two hours. That's how long she'd been waiting for him. The hour neared five o'clock in the morning, and she had yet to sleep a wink. Wringing her hands, she repressed the nausea burning in her stomach. Had she, in an attempt to fix a problem, only exacerbated it? Perhaps enlisting the help of a brothel Madame had not been the best idea.

She started when the noises she expected finally came, heralding Sheridan's arrival. Fighting the urge to run to him, she stayed rooted to the spot, facing the door separating their suites. She counted the seconds as he ascended the stairs, then entered his chamber. She could hear his deep voice, mingled with that of his valet, who he dismissed.

After a long while, she decided she'd delayed long enough. She'd spent far more time than she ought waiting for something to happen. She'd taken matters into her own hands tonight; there seemed no reason she couldn't not continue to do so.

She found her husband seated in a high-backed chair near his fireplace, the orange glow of flames playing over his patrician features. He wore only a pair of snug breeches, and smelled faintly of soap.

For a long while, he said nothing, nor did he so much as acknowledge her presence in the room. She stood just in front of him, so close the tips of her toes almost touched his.

At last, his gaze shifted to her.

"I owe you an apology," he began, his voice hoarse and thick.

She frowned. "You do?"

He nodded. "You must have found out, somehow, that I would go to that brothel tonight. Such knowledge hurt you, and you came after me, didn't you? What did Madame Petra do, what did she say, to convince you to go along with that … that …" He trailed off, shaking his head. "It doesn't matter. I should never have gone there, and I most certainly should not have been so indiscreet to allow you find out. And, it's the damndest thing, Cecily. If my father, or my uncles, or any other man of my acquaintance knew his wife had discovered his intention to go to a house of ill repute, he would not care about her feelings. He wouldn't give a damn if she were hurt, or angry. He would expect her to remain silent about it and go on performing her duties as his wife and blast all else. But, you see, I love you. I *care* about what you think of me. I would never want to do anything to cause you pain."

When he glanced up at her again, she could see he meant every word. His wounded expression caused pity to stab through her chest. Sinking down onto his knee, she took his head in her hands and lowered it to her breast. He rested there with a sigh, wrapping his arms around her and holding tight.

"You're right," she murmured, running a hand through his mussed hair. "I don't want you going back there."

He nodded, the stubble on his jaw rasping against the fabric of her dressing gown. "I won't, Cecily. I promise you."

Turning his face up, she gazed down into his eyes. "I want you to fulfill your every need and desire with me."

His fingers clenched the fabric of her robe. "You don't know how much I want to. I have fantasies, thoughts about the sort of things ... but, those things—"

"Made me feel alive," she interjected. "Tonight, you made love to me like I was a different woman."

"I thought you were a whore."

She smiled. "If that is what it is like, I think I would very much like for you to treat me like a whore."

He drew a sharp breath, starting as he glanced up at her. "You don't know what you're saying!"

Grasping his hands, she placed them flat on her body, covering them with her own and sliding them up over her breasts. His breath hitched, and his fingers curled around them. She arched her back and pushed them more fully into his palms.

"Did you like what you saw from the other side of that curtain, my love? Petra ... she is a beautiful woman."

His breath grew ragged as she sank onto his lap, straddling his thighs.

"Yes. She's almost as beautiful as you."

"I felt so wanton, knowing you sat on the other side of that veil, watching her do those wicked things to me. Do you know what would have made it even better?"

He lowered his head into the valley between her breasts, nudging the sides of her dressing gown apart as his fingers deftly untied the sash. "What?"

"To have your hands on me, too ... your mouth ... to feel you both at the same time, tasting me, touching me." She shivered when his fingers tweaked her nipples, applying gentle pressure. One of his thumbnails rasped the taut peak, drawing a gasp. "I saw how you looked at her. You want her, too."

He gripped her thighs, mouth latched onto one nipple as he grasped the hem of her nightgown and lifted it. "I had no idea you fancied other women."

Cecily's head fell back while his lips found her neck, his tongue rasping along the vital vein thrumming with her pulse. "I did not, either. When I asked for her help, and she suggested that we perform those acts to arouse you, I was shocked, to say the least. I had no idea such things were done."

One of his hands brushed the damp curls of her mons, and he reached between them, unfastening his breeches. He rested against her, powerful and thick, throbbing with arousal. She groaned and ground against it, pressing her wet inner folds against his cock.

"No more reticence," she whispered. He lifted her, then eased her down onto his erection, impaling her inch by slow inch. "I want you to feel free to do what you want with me, Sherry."

His hands trembled when they found her hips, taking them in a bruising grip.

"I want to," he murmured. "God, you don't know how hard it's been. I look at you and I see a sweet innocent, a lady ... *my* lady."

"Then close your eyes," she whispered, "and pretend I'm her."

He shook his head, refusing to break her gaze.

Pressing her hand over his eyes, she pushed his head back, forcing it to rest on the back of the chair.

"Cecily, stop this."

She moved against him, forcing a low moan from his throat. Smiling in satisfaction, she did it again, careful to keep her hand in place.

"Your cock feels so good inside me, my lord," she purred, imitating Petra's faint accent. "You want to fuck me, don't you? You want to take me from behind while I taste your wife's cunt."

He grunted, the muscles in his chest and abdomen tightening and contracting as she slid up and down the length of his rod.

"Hmmm, maybe I'll kiss you and give you a taste. You'd like that, too, wouldn't you, my lord? To taste your wife's sweet little quim on my lips."

Sheridan groaned, his hands palming her hips again and forcing her up and down harder, faster.

"Yes," he hissed from between gritted teeth.

Her head fell back again, and she allowed her hand to fall from over his eyes, satisfied that they would remain closed. She obeyed his silent command to go faster, gripping the back of his neck and hanging on as he bucked upward to meet her. She reveled in the power she'd discovered in her body, in her own womanhood. Never had she thought she could be so bold, so daring. The encounter at Madame Petra's had awakened her desires, as well as her curiosity. She wanted to discover all that could be learned about the bedroom arts.

Before this night, they'd only made love in one manner—with Sheridan on top of her, in the dark. This way, with him beneath her, her pleasure increased tenfold; each stroke of his cock inside her caressed a sensitive place deep within, one that brought on the telltale spasms she'd learned signaled her release.

She shattered, screaming so loud it was a wonder the servants didn't come running to ensure that someone wasn't killing her. His hand clapped over her mouth, but his assault on her body never ceased. His hips pumped upward, his breaths growing shorter and more ragged, until he groaned his own release, filling her with the hot gush of his seed.

He collapsed against the chair, sweat glistening on his bare skin, chest heaving from the exertion. She fell against him, cheek resting against his shoulder.

Now came the part she'd always enjoyed—the closeness she always felt with him when their lovemaking had ended. Instead, now, even that felt better because they were both more satisfied than they'd ever been.

Before she knew it, her eyelids drooped and she had drifted off to sleep. She didn't know how long they dozed, but when she came to, he was carrying her to the bed. The sun had long since risen, but with strict orders from the servants that they were not to be disturbed, Sheridan joined her in her bed, and they slept.

CHAPTER 6

When Sheridan awoke the next morning, the bed beside him lay empty. Yet, the pillow where his wife's head had rested still smelled of her. Despite the late hour they'd gone to bed, he felt surprisingly well-rested. The tension that had taken up residence in his joints and muscles had eased away. He'd slept better than he had in months.

A smile curved his mouth as he got off the mattress, stretching, glorying in the light of the sun filtering through the sheer lace curtains and warming his skin. Ringing for his valet, he slid on his robe and entered the dressing room with a spring in his step. If he hurried, he could find Cecily before she finished breakfast and left for the day. She and one of her numerous ladies' charity groups would be visiting poor families in Whitechapel to deliver baskets of necessary items to help the struggling lower class to survive. They'd spent months accumulating the items during the season, and the day would be important to her.

He suffered through a shave, but cried off when James remarked that his hair needed a trim. He didn't have time if he wanted to see

Cecily off. Enduring the valet's fussing, he allowed his mind to drift back over the explosive sexual encounter he'd enjoyed with his wife the night before. Who would have thought her sweet, innocent demeanor had hidden away an insatiable wanton? He did not know if his father had been wrong about gently-bred ladies, or if his wife simply proved a rare creature.

But, what if the entire thing had been an act? Perhaps Cecily had been led to believe she *had* to act like a wanton in order to hold his interest. Which would be the farthest thing from the truth. She had never needed wiles to capture him. He'd been ensnared from the moment he'd laid eyes upon her.

Scowling, he brushed James' fussy hands off and declared his appearance more than acceptable. Sending the man away, he studied his reflection with uncertainty. Her words came back to him in a rush, filling him with guilt.

I don't want you going back there.

His dear, sweet Cecily had done what she thought necessary to keep him from straying. Who could blame her? She had, in fact, caught him in a brothel. He tried to convince himself that he'd done nothing wrong because the whore he'd fucked had turned out to be his wife. Yet, a niggling thought in the back of his mind persisted—he hadn't known it was her. If Cecily hadn't been there, he might likely have slaked his lust on some other doxy.

She needed to be assured that his love for her, or his physical need, were not contingent upon her acting in a way that made her uncomfortable. It became even more imperative for him to speak with her.

A lady knows her place. She should never make demands of her husband. A man ought to do as he pleases, and a woman should never seek to tell him otherwise.

"Sod off, old man," he mumbled, ignoring the unwelcome voice of the viscount.

He nodded cordially to the maid who paused in dusting a mirror and set of sconces in the hall to curtsy. Striding for the stairs, he fought to remain outwardly dignified in front of the members of his household staff. It would not do for him to run, or take the stairs two at a time, or cry out Cecily's name as he tore through the house looking for her.

The dining room door hung open, and the lilt of feminine voices beckoned. He paused in the doorway, struck dumb by the sight that greeted him. His wife sat in her customary place, looking quite radiant in a white and blue muslin walking dress, her hair swept up in a soft, elegant arrangement. She poured tea for herself, and a guest—a woman whose low, throaty, accented voice sent a rush of blood straight to his groin.

That woman wore a walking dress in a shade of puce that would have made anyone else look like a drab. On her, the color enhanced the dusky hue of olive-toned skin and dark, shining hair falling just past her jaw in a soft shimmer of waves.

"Do you take sugar in your tea, Madame?" Cecily asked, her voice light and cordial, as if she hadn't stood in a bordello with this woman the night before and allowed her to taste her sweet little cunt.

The memory caused his breeches to become uncomfortably snug.

"Yes, two lumps, please," Petra answered in tones just as polite.

He watched them without moving from his place just within the doors, uncertain of how to approach such a situation. Not every day a man came down to breakfast to find his wife pouring tea for a brothel Madame. He became aware of the absence of servants, making him even more wary. Why had Petra come, and why had Cecily banished the servants to take breakfast with her? What the devil were they up to now?

"You may come in, my lord, and close the door as you do, please."

Sheridan started, his eyebrows jumping up toward his hairline at Petra's lofty command. In *his* home.

Frowning, he closed the door none too gently behind him, and strode forward. "See here—"

"Have a seat, darling." Cecily's soft blue eyes snapped up and locked with his, pleading silently. "Shall I serve you a plate? I dismissed the servants so we could speak in private, but I'm more than happy to see to the task. I know what you like."

For some reason, her last statement held the hint of a double entendre. Was it his imagination, or did her voice grow huskier as she'd said it?

"Talk?" he murmured, glancing up to find Petra staring at him. "What is there to discuss?"

His wife had already left her place at the table and taken up an empty plate from the sideboard. As she filled it, Petra speared him with a knowing glance.

"The rules, my lord."

He wrinkled his brow. "Rules?"

"Of our liaison—you, your wife, and myself. If we are to continue past last night, I must inform you of how I like to do things."

Understanding finally dawned.

"Ah, well ... there seems to have been some sort of misunderstanding. Last evening's encounter need not be repeated."

Her full, decadent lips curved into a smirk. "Oh, no, my lord. We shall find many other ways to enjoy each other."

As he blustered and stammered, searching for an appropriate response, Cecily returned with his plate.

A throaty laugh fell from Petra's lips. "Cecily, darling, did you not inform your husband that you have hired me?"

Roses bloomed upon his wife's cheeks and she lowered her eyes. "We began talking about it, but ..." she cleared her throat. "We became distracted."

The Madame's lips parted in a wicked grin. "Then our session last night was a success, no?"

He turned to his wife, ignoring the plate she'd set before him. His appetite had long since fled.

"Darling, I do believe you and I need a word alone. I suppose you are under the impression that I wish for you to do things which are distasteful to you in order to please me."

Brow knit in confusion, she reached across the table and took his hand.

"My love, I think you are the one who has misunderstood. Did you not hear me when I told you I wanted more for us? That I wanted to explore beyond the things we did last night?"

His mouth fell open, but words did not come forth for several seconds. Shaking his head, he tried again.

"I … I did hear you. Quite clearly. But you … you meant it?"

She gave him a radiant smile. "Of course I did. I did not just come to Madame Petra's last night to bring you home. I went to enlist her help. Her services come highly recommended, from what I gathered. I believe she can help us with our little … predicament."

He felt uncertain of whether he should ask her who had referred her to the Madame, deciding to focus on the obvious questions for the moment.

"What predicament?"

"You are uptight, my lord," Petra said, lifting the teacup to her lips. Taking a sip, she hummed in appreciation.

His jaw clenched, and annoyance flared his nostrils. "I beg your pardon?"

She set the tea into its saucer and folded her hands on the table.

"Let us dispense with nonsense, Sheridan. The fact of the matter is, your wife hired me to assist you in injecting a dose of much-needed joy into your intimate life. Like most men of the *ton*, you are under the misguided impression that the lady you married is not a woman with sexual needs and desires similar to your own. You have handled her like a porcelain doll, when what she really wants is for you to treat her like a *woman*.

"Now, I am expensive, but that is because I'm good. I have worked with many couples of the *ton*, and I have never failed a single one. Together, the three of us will explore the boundaries of your intimate relationship and attempt to establish new ones. We will also seek to find the root of your problem, because based upon what I saw last night, your issue is not a physical one. It is all in your mind.

"That is why I am here. To guide you. To participate, if you want me to. It is not something I do with every couple, but your wife seemed to enjoy it, so I see no need to deprive her, or you. Let us enrich your married life. Oh, and I must inform you that I am regularly inspected by a physician to ensure that I am clean. I also take precautions to avoid conception. You need not worry, I am a Madame worth her salt. We begin now, if you do not mind. I am a busy woman."

For a moment, silence reigned in the dining room. Petra sat staring at him in quiet challenge. Cecily regarded him anxiously. He tapped his fingers against the table, staring back and forth between them both.

So the Madame was at their disposal. The sexual aspect of such an arrangement intrigued him. It appealed to him. However, having her attempt to counsel him in other areas, he could have done without. He knew good and well where his problem lay, and did not wish to discuss it with his wife, or her.

"What if I say no?" he asked, breaking the silence. "What if I decide that my marriage doesn't need interference from you?"

"Then you would be making a very big mistake," she said.

Glancing at his wife, he could see this meant a lot to her. Without the haze of exhaustion or too much brandy clouding his judgment, he now clearly understood that she'd meant every word of what she'd said to him the past night.

"I would do anything for you," he said, drawing her gaze up from the tablecloth. "If you believe it necessary, I will participate."

She exhaled, a sigh of relief. "Oh, Sherry, really?"

He nodded. "Perhaps Petra is right. I do have … notions which are hard to forget."

Petra stood, removing a silver timepiece from the pocket of her gown and observing the time. "We will discuss that at length, but not today. I believe Cecily must depart within the hour and I have an appointment, as well, with a modiste. Before I leave, however, I do believe you should eat your breakfast, my lord."

He frowned down at his still-full plate. The eggs had grown cold, and his appetite had still not returned.

"I'm not hungry."

She rounded the table, hips swaying beneath her gown.

"Do the offerings on your plate not tickle your fancy? Pity." Taking the plate, she placed it on the sideboard. "Cecily, darling, will you clear the table?"

His wife rose, complying silently. Yet, a glimmer of mischief shone in her eyes, and he began to feel like an antelope trapped by two voracious lionesses.

"If you are not interested in food, we must find something else to tempt you with, mustn't we, Cecily?"

She murmured her agreement, coming to stand beside Petra next to his chair.

He remained in his seat, staring up at the two beautiful vixens standing before him. His breath hitched when Petra took his wife's face in her hands and leaned in for a kiss. Cecily's lips parted and her velvety, pink tongue met the other woman's. His cock immediately filled with blood, and the organ fought for freedom against the front of his breeches.

Petra cupped Cecily's breasts, giving them a gentle squeeze. Tilting his wife's head back, she lowered her own and trailed her tongue from the valley between her breasts, up to the vein where her pulse thrummed. Cecily's soft moan made his bollocks contract, rendering his arousal all the more urgent.

They shifted until Cecily's back had turned toward him.

"Help your wife disrobe, my lord," Petra said, her voice low and throaty as she continued squeezing and kneading Cecily's breasts.

He knit his brow. "Here? Now?"

Petra stared at him over his wife's shoulder as he stood.

"Our first lesson, my lord. I know you were likely taught to only make love to your wife in the evening, in her bed, with the candles snuffed out."

Embarrassment heated his neck when he realized the majority of their encounters had been just that.

"This is your wife," Petra continued. "She is yours to enjoy whenever, wherever, and whatever way you please. Spontaneity, my lord. Our first lesson."

Excitement coursed through him, heating his blood and filling his ears with a dull roar. Pushing his chair aside, he stepped forward until his body brushed Cecily's, the soft curves of her buttocks fitting perfectly against his groin. His hands shook as he lifted them to begin unfastening the back of her gown.

With a satisfied nod, the Madame returned her attention to Cecily. Catching the lobe of her ear between her teeth, she suckled gently before beginning to nibble on the side of her neck.

The gown began to sag as it loosened, and her fichu fluttered to the carpet, forgotten. His hands caressed the curves of her waist and hips as he pushed the dress to the floor. She stepped from it, and Petra took it up, laying it neatly over the back of a chair. Taking her place in front of Cecily once more, she hooked her forefinger into the neckline of his wife's chemise and lowered it to reveal one plump breast, then the other.

His hips moved, causing friction between his hard cock and her soft derriere, while his hands slid up over her corset and toward the tits perfectly cradled and lifted by the undergarment. She shivered when he squeezed them with an urgency that stole gentleness from his touch. She didn't seem to mind. In fact, the harder he squeezed, and the more insistently he tugged on her nipples, the faster her breath raced and the louder her moans became.

Petra bent to take one of the perky, pink nipples into her mouth, tearing a moan from deep in his throat at the sight. Cecily's hips bucked, and the Madame moved closer, tightly pressing her between them.

He lifted Cecily's breasts to the Madame's mouth, massaging them while she feasted, her darting tongue circling the pink tips. Not to be outdone, he lowered his head and latched onto the side of her neck. His teeth scraped the taut tendons and his tongue caressed her beating pulse, eliciting another shiver and soft sigh of delight.

"Lay her on the table, my lord," Petra whispered, raising her head from his wife's heaving breasts. "I want a proper taste."

Turning Cecily to face him, he captured her mouth and wrapped his arms around her waist. Their tongues mated while he lifted her, setting her on the wood surface as instructed.

Grasping his arm, Petra knelt before the table and took him with her. She lifted the hem of Cecily's chemise, revealing soft, creamy thighs and the naked triangle of curls between them. His mouth went dry when he realized she'd foregone wearing drawers.

The scent of her arousal filled his nostrils, and the golden curls covering her mons had become damp with the evidence. He reached down and applied pressure to his aching cock, desperate for release. However, he was too intrigued to discover where this might lead. So he restrained himself.

"So sweet," Petra murmured, leaning forward to press a kiss to Cecily's inner thigh.

He stroked her calf, letting his palm skim over her knee and the top of her stocking. His thumb massaged her other thigh, steadily working toward her core. Petra's slender fingers parted her curls, revealing the tender flesh within. His searching thumb came to rest on the swollen bud nestled within the folds. The gentle pressure elicited a shiver, and then a moan when he circled the digit, smearing her in her own honey.

He repeated the motion, hypnotized by the sight of his thumb stroking over the hot, wet flesh. With a low sigh of appreciation, Petra leaned forward and ran her tongue over the folds beneath his stroking thumb, then circled her opening. Cecily cried out, gripping the table-cloth in her fists. The Madame continued her erotic ministrations, the sound of her suckling and licking his wife's wet cunt filling the room. Tearing his eyes away from where his hand met Cecily's body, he allowed his gaze to fall to the swell of Petra's breasts, heaving against the neckline of her gown.

She'd said she was to be enjoyed, hadn't she?

Deciding that he very much wanted another glimpse of her sumptuous tits, he reached back and unfastened several of the tiny buttons running down her spine. She arched her back, offering her breasts to him as the front of her gown sagged to her waist. The thumb of his right hand quickened, continuing to stroke Cecily's clit. His left hand slid down the front of Petra's chemise and closed around a perky breast. The nipple leapt to attention at his touch, stiffening between his fingers.

She whimpered, but never ceased in her own actions, her tongue lapping at the honey seeping from Cecily's entrance. One of her hands found the front of his breeches, and he hissed as she caressed his cock through the fabric.

"Yes," he growled, thrusting against her questing hand.

She gave him another bold caress, then rubbed lower, squeezing his bollocks.

Snatching the garment open, he freed his member and watched it fall into her hand. Her fingers closed around him and stroked rhythmically. Her palm felt soft and warm, her grip firm, creating the perfect amount of friction. Resting his head against Cecily's thigh, he closed his eyes, groaning as the hand around his cock stroked faster.

The scent of her arousal overwhelmed him, and he longed to taste her for himself. Gripping Petra's hair firmly, he pulled her away and availed himself of her lips. Her mouth was plump and ripe, perfect for kissing. Even better, they tasted of his sweet Cecily, slick with his wife's arousal, and he found the flavor dancing on her tongue, as well.

Pulling away, he turned his attention to the cunt spread out on the table before him. Parting her lower lips, he latched onto her pearl, suckling with gentle insistence. Cecily screamed, her back arching and causing her hips to thrust against his mouth. He devoured her, his lips and tongue drawing even more wetness to seep from her core.

Petra found her way in, her tongue darting between Cecily's

buttocks and trailing upward, lapping at the trickle of moisture that had escaped Sheridan's hungry mouth. Their tongues touched and caressed one another, Cecily's tender pink flesh between them. On the table, his wife squirmed and writhed, crying out her pleasure. The Madame's hand left his cock, and she lifted it to thrust two fingers into his wife's welcoming sheath.

"Oh my," she murmured, taking up a rhythmic stroke within Cecily's channel. "I can feel her throbbing, my lord. She's so close."

"Yes," Cecily whimpered, hips thrusting wildly against Petra's questing fingers and his devouring mouth. "Heavens, that feels so good."

Her words only further exacerbated his own need. She enjoyed this. His wife was a passionate, responsive creature.

"Come for us, darling," he murmured.

She trembled, then shook and fell apart. Muffling her screams with the back of her hand, she rode Petra's fingers and his tongue to completion.

As he lapped at Cecily's weeping cunt, he faintly realized that the other woman had ceased pumping her fingers inside of her channel. Taking up where she'd left off, he pressed first one, then a second finger into Cecily's sheath. Slick, wet heat enveloped him at the moment the same thing happened to his cock.

Gasping in shock, he felt the muscles of his abdomen contract, nearly knocking him to his back on the carpet as Petra's mouth and tongue stroked him in a rapid, merciless rhythm. Moaning against the cunt pressed to his lips, he closed his eyes and held on to Cecily for dear life. Never could he have imagined a pleasure so intoxicating—the feel of one woman's mouth wrapped around his cock, while the taste of another fueled the fires of his lust.

In his youth, he'd experienced the mouths of many whores, but none as skilled as Petra. She suckled him as if starving, her tongue stroking and teasing the ridged underside of his member while her fingers fondled and squeezed his tender bollocks.

His fingers quickened within Cecily, coaxing her arousal to life again with him using his digits to fuck her in the same rhythm with which Petra sucked his cock. His wife hurtled toward release again, her thighs trembling on either side of him as she fisted the tablecloth once more and rested her bare feet on his shoulders.

She reached her peak at the same time he groaned and shuddered, his seed spurting into Petra's mouth.

His tense muscles melted, and a languid sort of fatigue dropped over him. Cecily fell limp and silent on the table, her bared breasts heaving as she fought to catch her breath.

Petra deftly tucked his cock back into his smallclothes and fastened his breeches. The two worked together to set Cecily to rights.

He helped her to her feet and straightened her chemise. Petra held her gown while she stepped into it, then gave him her back as she buttoned Cecily's dress. He buttoned the Madame, allowing his fingertips to linger on the back of her neck when he pushed a stray lock of hair aside.

The encounter had been more satisfying than he'd imagined. His wildest fantasies could not have compared. Cecily had been right last night when she'd teased him by guessing at his secret thoughts. He *did* want to fuck Petra from behind, watching as she drove his wife to the heights of pleasure with her perfect, skilled mouth. He clenched his teeth, balling his hand into a fist at his side to keep from snatching her skirts up and making his dream a reality then and there.

His wife had paid a king's ransom to retain Petra for them, which meant there would be plenty of time to have them both in every way he could think of before it would all end. He'd never thought he wanted a mistress, but thinking of sharing one with his wife became an intriguing notion. Damn the costs—Cecily had touched very little of her dowry, and if this made her happy, he was glad to oblige her. After all, he benefited in the process.

As Petra bid them both goodbye, leaving them in the dining room with her promise to return soon, he gazed down at his wife and smiled. She looked radiant—eyes wide, bright, and shining with a secret only he and Petra could know, cheeks flushed pink from exertion, skin glowing like a woman who'd been thoroughly loved.

At that moment, he had a hard time remembering why he'd protested this arrangement in the first place. Who could have known bringing another woman into their intimate life would have made his prim, proper little wife so content?

CHAPTER 7

"**W**hat's gotten into you?"

Cecily turned to Penelope and smiled. "Whatever do you mean?"

Even as she asked, a giggle bubbled in her throat. Her step was light—downright springy, even—and a cheerful hum had been dancing on her tongue all afternoon.

They walked the dirty streets in one of London's most despicable slums; yet, for all her cheer, one would have thought she strolled the verdant expanse of Hyde Park.

"You're humming," her friend observed aloud, eyeing her incredulously. "And you're … good heavens, you're *skipping*!"

Glancing down at her calfskin boots, she grinned. "So I am. And why shouldn't I hum and skip? Our many months of raising funds and gathering items for the needy have paid off. Today, we get to see their smiling faces while we give them their baskets, and it's such a glorious spring day, besides."

Lady Mary Anne Willoughby poked her head between them with a laugh, thrusting her basket through the gap she'd created and linking each of her arms through theirs. Her basket swung against her hip, then Cecily's as they continued on at a steady pace.

"It's more than that," Mary Ann said with a sly grin. "It takes more than a sunny afternoon of charitable work to put a glow like that upon a woman's face. Mr. Cranfield must be quite the randy stallion."

The two exploded into a paroxysm of giggles, while Penelope shushed them and glanced around to ensure none of the others had overheard them. They were in the company of twenty other ladies— members of the Mayfair Ladies' Charitable Society—and ten gentle-men. Several husbands and brothers had been coerced into coming along to protect them from street urchins and pickpockets.

"Do you *want* everyone to hear you talking like a Haymarket strumpet?" Penelope hissed, her voice a low whisper.

"Oh, do calm down," Mary Anne scoffed. "There's no one here but us." Turning back to Cecily, she lowered her voice. "Do tell me every-thing, darling. Is he wonderful?"

Cecily thought of Sheridan's long fingers thrusting between her legs, his cock doing the same as she straddled him, and a blush heated her face.

"He's everything I ever imagined," she whispered, "and more."

"I knew he was a good sort," Mary Ann replied. "I can always tell."

"Yes, because you've so much experience when it comes to men," Penelope grumbled.

"I've got more than you," Mary Anne retorted, her voice dripping with syrupy sweet venom.

Like Cecily, she was newly married and seemed to be enjoying her status as a countess and a wife.

Frowning, Cecily observed Penelope from the corner of her eye. Her friend was even surlier than usual. She'd always been opinionated on the subject of men—even seemed to hold them in very low regard —but today, it appeared to have reached a new level of hatred.

"I am happy for you, darling," Mary Anne whispered so only the two of them could hear. "A happy marriage is the one thing a young lady has to hope for, is it not?"

A happy marriage, yes. A passionate one.

She could hardly wait to learn what Petra would teach them. As well, she could not wait to learn more about her husband and the reasons behind his stiffness and reticence. As much as she loved him, she was all too aware of the fact that their speedy courtship hadn't given them time to get to know one another. They had their entire lives for that. Yet, something told her that learning more about her husband on an intellectual level would only deepen their intimacy—which had been her ultimate goal in hiring Madame Petra.

Cecily threw herself into her busy day, losing track of time as she and her ladies went from home to home, delivering baskets and luxuriating in the joy they'd brought to the unfortunate. By the end of the afternoon, her feet had grown sore and she felt exhausted, but nothing could wipe the smile from her face.

She arrived home just in time to begin dressing for the Morley's ball. She could hear Sheridan chatting with his valet through the door separating his dressing room from hers. Deciding to give him a bit of privacy, she kept to her room to prepare for the night. Taking her time, she enjoyed a long, languid soak in the tub while her lady's maid prepared her gown and accessories.

The ensemble she'd chosen was unlike anything she'd ever worn. Yet, Petra had insisted on it.

"You must show your husband that he is married to a woman," she'd said when they'd covered the subject of Cecily's clothing. "Not a porcelain doll. A woman who knows how to accentuate her best assets commands notice. Sheridan will be unable to keep his hands off you."

Grinning at her reflection, she decided the Madame had been right. She hadn't even donned her gown yet, and already, she felt like the most decadent, sensual creature in the world. The items Petra had given her were the height of French fashion in ladies' undergarments. A corset of black satin cupped and lifted her breasts in a display that would leave her husband salivating—Petra, too, she realized, as the Madame had confessed to enjoying her breasts. A silk chemise edged in black lace felt like heaven against her bare bottom. Going without drawers had seemed naughty, but she enjoyed the way the silk felt against her skin and the way her thighs teased her mons when she walked. Black stockings, edged in crimson lace and bows, completed her secret ensemble.

Her gown boasted the same shade of scarlet, with a neckline so daring her nipples would be sure to make an appearance if she so much as sneezed. She clasped a black diamond choker around her neck, a piece from the Cranfield family collection, and matched it with a pair of earrings bearing the same stones. Black silk gloves covered her arms to the elbow. Her maid had styled her hair in a soft arrangement of loose curls, leaving several to rest over one creamy shoulder. It teased the eye, inviting lips to kiss her exposed collarbone and travel lower.

Taking up her matching reticule, she descended to meet Sheridan in the lobby.

He stood waiting at the foot of the stairs, one hand braced on the mahogany balustrade, his head lowered. The candlelight caused his hair to gleam like brilliant gold and the diamond pin situated in the frothy white linen of his cravat to twinkle.

Clearing her throat, she struck a pose at the top of the staircase and waited for him to notice her.

Green eyes lifted and found her, widening while taking in her appearance from head to toe. His gaze smoldered while she began to descend, giving her hips an exaggerated sway. His nostrils flared, and his chest swelled as he ascended the last few steps and offered his arm to assist her the rest of the way down.

"Good evening, Sherry." She smiled up at him.

He did not smile back, but then, he didn't have to. His gaze spoke volumes, as did the bulging bicep beneath her hand and the quickened breath she detected.

He'd grown aroused.

Her husband looked gorgeous in his black evening clothes, a silver satin waistcoat relieving the dark color. He'd been freshly shaved, but had foregone a haircut. His golden locks almost swept his shoulders now, and Cecily found she liked the rakish, masculine appeal the longer hair gave him.

"Good evening, my love," he murmured, raising her hand to his lips for a kiss.

His mouth lingered and his fingers tightened around hers, possessive.

"You are an absolute vision," he said, placing her hand back on his arm. "I will be the envy of every man present."

The butler opened the front door to reveal their waiting carriage. A footman appeared with his greatcoat and hat and her cloak. Once properly attired, Sheridan led her out into the night and toward the waiting conveyance.

Another footman opened the door and handed her up. The door closed once Sheridan had climbed in behind her, and within moments, they were underway.

She'd never felt so excited about attending a ball. Yet, as the carriage rocked and swayed, carrying them closer to their destination, she experienced a tiny thrill at the notion of what the end of the night could bring.

They arrived at the perfect time—not so early that they were forced to stand in the receiving line overlong, nor too far past fashionably late. The low buzz of conversation seemed to swell as they descended into the ballroom, causing Sheridan to smirk.

"I do believe you've caused quite a stir with your mode of dress, my love," he murmured.

She glanced up at him. "Are you displeased, husband?"

"On the contrary. As you enter on my arm, no man here can take his eyes from you."

She raised her eyebrows. "And you *want* that?"

He led her to the dance floor while the strains of the first waltz filled the ballroom. She had eyes only for him as he drew her close and awaited the music.

"Let them look," he murmured. "Let them all look and know that you belong to me. They will languish to know you could never belong to them."

"You're an arrogant show-off," she said, laughing.

"And you're a tease," he whispered before swinging her into the first steps of the waltz.

Losing herself in the music and the moment, she allowed her husband to carry her away in his arms. It would not do for them to dance together more than twice this evening, and her next waltz would likely be claimed the moment they parted. This would be the only time tonight when they could hold each other this close. It could be a prelude to what would come once they returned home.

By the time the dance ended, Cecily salivated for it. Since she'd been introduced to pleasure, she couldn't seem to get enough.

Lifting her gloved hand, he placed a kiss upon the back of it and gave her a knowing smile. "Until later, my dear."

They parted ways—she to find her friends for gossip and chatter between dances, he to sign a few dance cards and engage in some obligatory dances before retreating to the gaming room. Finding her fan, she opened it and employed it against the stifling heat. The ball could already be hailed a success based upon the crush filling every available inch of the room.

Wafting her fan languidly, she gazed about her, searching for Penelope in the crowd. Frowning, she noticed that the murmur she'd caused when entering the ballroom had not faded. In fact, it seemed to have increased now that she stood alone. A lump of panic rose in her throat as she turned in a slow circle, now acutely aware of the many pairs of eyes boring into her. Hands hiding behind gloves and fans, the members of the *ton* whispered about something ... something involving her.

Her gown wasn't *that* scandalous. She was married now, besides, and could certainly dress as a mature woman without being gossiped about.

Her heart began to pound as she realized something had gone horribly wrong. The ladies present gave her a wide berth when they passed her, a few even going so far as to lift their skirts to keep them from touching hers. Several gentlemen watched her like hawks, their gazes openly salacious, as if they saw her as a fallen woman ripe for conquest.

"Sherry," she whispered, looking for her husband.

He couldn't have gone far; yet, she felt so utterly trapped and alone with so many eyes upon her, as though an entire canyon separated them.

Holding her head high, she began to move, testing her theory. Sure enough, a wide circle of empty space seemed to surround her wherever she went, with people going out of their way to avoid contact with her.

Typically, her dance card became full within minutes of stepping into any ballroom. Yet, tonight, it remained empty. She spotted Mary Anne nearby, along with several other members of her ladies' society group. Smiling, she made her way toward them. These women were her friends—surely, they would greet her and tell her what had the *ton* in such a tizzy.

Yet, when she approached, several fans snapped up to cover gossiping mouths. Eyes shifted to avoid her gaze, and curls bounced as heads turned, dismissing her. Gasping, she backed away from them, hurt and betrayal stinging her like the lash of a whip.

Dear God, what had she done to deserve such treatment?

Turning, she found herself face to face with Penelope, who breathed heavily, as if she'd elbowed her way from across the ballroom to meet her.

Her chin trembled and tears stung her eyes.

"Don't," Penelope whispered, taking her arm and forcing a false smile. "Do not cry. Not here. Come with me."

She was right. To break down in front of them would only fuel the fires of gossip, and Cecily didn't even know what had caused it yet. Raising her chin an inch, she allowed her friend to guide her toward a set of double doors leading out into the garden. The terrace beyond it stood empty. There, they could speak in private.

The seconds it took them to reach the terrace felt like hours, creeping by as the bit of theater taking place within the ballroom continued.

The dull hum of gossip faded away once they cleared the doors, finding sweet relief in the cool air of the evening.

She turned to Penelope the moment they were alone.

"I don't understand. What is going on?"

Penelope's dark eyes had turned grave, her mouth a pinched line. "That, my dear, is what we call the cut direct. You just received it from half the *ton*."

She shook her head, brow creased in disbelief. "But ... *why?*"

Her friend began to pace, seeming to have not heard her question. She sighed, hands clasped behind her back.

"Why did you do it, Cecily? Did I not tell you that married men indulged in such pastimes behind their wives' backs? What could have possessed you to go find out for yourself? Now, you might well be ruined!"

"What on Earth are you talking about?"

Agitation made her tone short and curt and caused sweat to coat her palms beneath her gloves. What had felt like a dream just that afternoon became a nightmare by the second.

"Someone saw you, Cecily," Penelope replied, pausing in her pacing and turning to face her. "Coming and going from Madame Petra's in the dead of night."

A strangled sound escaped her throat despite the vise gripping it, preventing her from speaking.

"No well-bred woman would be caught dead in such an establishment," her friend continued. "Yet, you were seen, and someone has ousted you. Now gossip is swirling about what you might have been doing there. The speculation ranges from the obscene to the bizarre. It is not good, darling."

She squeezed her eyes closed, her mind filling with images of Petra on her knees, her lips and tongue coaxing wet heat from her cunt.

Embarrassment filled her and she realized she was well and truly ruined.

"I … I didn't do anything wrong," she protested meekly.

Penelope came forward, taking her hands and squeezing them gently, her expression full of pity.

"I know. You went after him because you felt betrayed, and you had every right to. Oh, but why couldn't you have waited to confront him at home? His reputation would not have been ruined by his presence in that place, but yours may well have been."

She shook her head, no longer able to fight the tears cascading down her cheeks. "I never meant for this to happen."

"Of course you didn't."

Penelope held her, hugging her tight. Clinging to her friend, she choked back a sob, realizing what this all meant for her. She would be shunned everywhere. No one would want a woman who consorted with whores to attend their parties, teas, or balls. No one would want to speak to her in Hyde Park, or invite her into their home, or allow their gently-bred, virginal daughters anywhere near her. And her charity groups …

"The society," she choked.

Penelope shook her head. "They've designated me to inform you that you are no longer welcome."

Dashing at her tears, she forced herself to take a deep breath. "You shouldn't be seen talking to me, Penelope. You should go back in there and ignore me, along with everyone else. There is no need for your reputation to suffer, as well."

"To hell with them all," Penelope declared, wiping her hands together as if ridding them of bothersome dust. "I have always been my own person, and you know this more than anyone else. I am a spinster with no desire to marry—thus making me a bit of an oddity and an outcast as it is. It makes sense that I would count a salacious whore among my friends."

Amusement pulled at the corners of her lips, and she couldn't hold back the laugh that shook her shoulders.

"Oh, you do know how to make me feel better. A spinster and a whore—we make quite a pair, do we not?"

Penelope's face grew serious again. "What do you need? I want to help you."

Cecily sighed. "Just one thing. I want to go home. I need Sheridan."

"Of course. Wait here."

Penelope retreated, leaving her alone. Without her friend there to feed her confidence, her shoulders deflated and tears filled her eyes again.

Why hadn't she been more discreet? Of course, she'd known she took a risk in going to Madame Petra's, but she would never have guessed someone would see and recognize her.

What had begun as a desire to breathe life into her monotonous marriage now threatened everything. Sheridan would be furious when he learned of the gossip making the rounds. He would blame her for the position he was now in. His peers would shun him, and his voice in the House of Lords had now been discredited. His father, the viscount, would not take this lightly. It would be just like him to cut off Sheridan's funds over such a scandal, leaving them in dire straits. Her dowry could only go so far.

Yes, she felt sure he would blame her, and could not fault him for that. She had ruined absolutely everything.

CHAPTER 8

heir townhouse was in an uproar when Sheridan and Cecily returned home. Annoyance and confusion gripped him when he found a large, over-embellished coach with the Perth crest waiting out front, and the vestibule filled with their trunks. It became exacerbated when he spied his father, standing with one foot propped on the bottom stair, observing his timepiece and pretending not to notice their entrance.

"Sheridan?" Cecily called, voice quivering.

"Go upstairs," he said. "I will determine what this is all about."

She seemed reluctant, but did what he asked, walking silently to the staircase and retaining the dignified set of her shoulders as she breezed past his father.

There hadn't been time for them to discuss what had happened at the Morley's ball, and now, it would have to wait even longer. When the viscount demanded an audience, he was not to be ignored.

Baldwin Cranfield III, Viscount of Perth, appeared like a mirror image of Sheridan, with only a little gray hair and the lines of age to distinguish him. He cut an imposing figure in his evening attire, his expression even sourer than usual. Unlike his son, he did not possess an easygoing nature. The viscount liked to control everyone and everything around him—including his adult son and his wife. Thus, the reason for his visit and the packed bags.

"You will depart for Edenwhite," he said in a clipped tone that warned he would tolerate no argument.

Sheridan bit back a scathing retort. He knew he walked a tightrope with his father, who had the power to cripple him financially.

"There is no need," he replied, clasping his hands behind his back. "The rumors about Cecily aren't true. If we remain and present a united front, the tongue-wagging will cease. If we don't give them anything more to talk about, they'll latch on to some new bit of nonsense and forget about my wife."

"Your *wife*." Baldwin shook his head, nostrils flaring as he seemed to fight to control his own anger. "It would seem we were mistaken about her. However, milk spilled cannot be put back in the bottle. We must weather this until it has passed."

He clenched his hands into fists at his sides, his fingernails biting into his palms. "Cecily is innocent here. I'll thank you not to speak ill of my wife while standing inside of my house."

"A house my money pays for," the viscount reminded him, arching one blond eyebrow. "If you'd disciplined your wife as I taught you—"

"You seem to have forgotten, I am no longer a child," he interrupted. "You might have forced me to do your bidding when I was young, but how I treat my wife is not subject to your approval, or your dictates."

"No," the viscount agreed. "But where you live is. You will remain at Edenwhite through the season. Perhaps when you return next year, you'll have sired a brat on the chit. That should keep her occupied."

Sheridan gritted his teeth, but couldn't bite the words back quick enough. "No."

His father straightened, tension squaring his shoulders. "No?"

"You heard me. I said no. Cecily and I will remain here for the season, and thank you to keep your nose out of our affairs."

Baldwin crossed his arms over his chest and gave his son a derisive smirk. "This united front you spoke of … I suppose you think your stepmother and I will play some part in it? The Viscount of Perth, shielding his heir from the cruelty of gossip and scorn."

Sheridan *had* counted on his father's influence to see them through this time, but realized now he shouldn't have. The viscount had always been a stickler for propriety, thus the many lessons in how one should expect one's wife to behave.

"I won't involve myself, since you have commanded me to stay out of your affairs," he continued when Sheridan didn't answer. "Neither will your brother or stepmother. I won't allow it."

He had no doubt of that. He also knew his family would never go against the viscount. His brother, the second son, barely clung to the fringe of their father's good graces. Their stepmother, a young chit of an age with Cecily, did not have a defiant bone in her body—thus the reason the viscount had chosen her.

"Do what you must," Sheridan replied, shrugging. "I will do the same."

Baldwin studied him in silence for a moment, anger and frustration emanating from him in tangible waves. After a while, he nodded, as if coming to a decision.

"I still expect you to vacate the premises," he declared. "If you wish to carry on without my influence, you shall do so without my money. I expect you gone by morning, or you are cut off. If you plan to go against me, I do hope you've been wise with your bride's dowry."

Retrieving his coat and hat from a footman, he left through the open door, which the butler closed behind him as he descended the front steps.

Ignoring the curious stares of the servants, Sheridan turned and made his way up the stairs.

His valet sat in the dressing room, giving various servants rebellious glares while they rifled through Sheridan's things. He shot to his feet when his master entered, panic widening his eyes and anger setting his jaw.

"I told them I would have no part in it, but they carried on without me. I warned them you would not like anyone but me packing your things, and that I would not do so unless I heard the order from your mouth. They proceeded to go against my wishes, and have likely ruined your shirts and cravats with their careless handling."

He fought back a smirk. James could always be trusted to fly into a tizzy over shirts and cravats no matter the situation.

"It's all right, James," he said. "Have you seen my wife?"

"In her chambers," James replied, "changing into her traveling clothes. Is it true that we are departing for Edenwhite?"

Sheridan felt one of his hands curling into a fist. Not the first time this evening he'd felt like punching something. Without answering the question, he passed through the door separating his dressing room from hers, then entered her chamber.

She sat in an armchair near the fire, hands folded in her lap. She'd changed into a demure carriage dress, and a small valise rested at her feet. His heart wrenched when her tear-filled eyes lifted to meet his.

Forcing a smile, he came farther into the room. Dismissing her maid, he knelt in front of her chair and took her hands in his.

"What's this?" he asked, nodding toward the valise.

"I am ready to leave," she replied.

Reaching up, he swiped away a tear with his thumb.

"We are not going anywhere."

Shaking her head, she stood. "I heard your father, Sherry. Every word. We cannot afford to remain here more than a few weeks without your allowance. Besides, perhaps he is right. The best thing to do is leave until the gossip blows over."

"But what about your ladies' group and your charity work? You were so excited about coming before the start of the season."

She sobbed, falling against him and burying her face against his chest. "They don't want me anywhere near them! They asked Penelope to inform me that I am no longer welcome."

Anger rose up in him as he held her, wracking his brain for a solution to their problem. He felt helpless enough as things stood, relying on the mercy of a man who required complete obedience from him in all matters. This, along with the fact that his wife had been forced to hire a whore in order to coax him to making love to her properly, made him feel inadequate.

"I'm so sorry," he murmured, kissing the top of her head. "This is all my fault."

"No," she protested, backing away from him. "I am the one who got caught leaving a brothel. I should never have been there, and now our friends will shun us, and your father will disown you ... all because I couldn't leave well enough alone."

"That's enough," he chided, grasping her shoulders. "Listen to me, Cecily. I've been a fool. I let my father control me once; I won't do it again."

She frowned. "What do you mean?"

"His *teachings* ... I let them influence our marriage, and it resulted in you not being happy with our intimate life. You acted out of desperation, and one could hardly blame you. Now that I understand what a passionate nature you have, I can't help but wonder how you went so long without saying something." He laughed. "Or beating me over the head with your parasol."

She giggled. "I felt tempted, I must admit. Still, I could have talked to you about the matter. I employed less conventional means, and now, we are ruined because of it."

"Half the women of the *ton* wish they had your courage, and the majority of the men wish their wives did, as well. Never apologize for what you did to make me see the light." He reached down and gripped one of her plump buttocks, giving it a squeeze. "I certainly enjoyed it."

Her lips curved into a smirk. "Too bad it has to end now. Petra and I had not yet finished with you."

An idea struck him so suddenly, he could hardly believe he hadn't thought of it before.

He smiled. "Maybe it doesn't have to end. Not yet."

Her brows scrunched quizzically. "What do you mean?"

Glad he hadn't taken off his coat, he gave her a quick kiss on the cheek and turned for the door.

"Don't take off your travelling clothes just yet. We are leaving when I return."

"Very well, but where are you going right now?"

He paused in the doorway, turning back to give her a smile. "It's a surprise. Trust me, you'll like it."

CHAPTER 9

Sheridan allowed his gaze to linger on the woman framed in the doorway that separated his and Cecily's room from hers. She'd freshened up, changing from her rumpled carriage dress to a simple black peignoir and matching wrapper. Let loose from its chignon, her lustrous, mahogany hair fell around her face in luscious waves.

Near the fire, Cecily reclined in the bath, head thrown back against the rim and eyes closed.

From where he stood, it proved difficult to ascertain whether or not she slept. She had to have been as exhausted as he had, after their sleepless night followed by a full day of travel.

Deciding to leave had been a good idea. Especially since he'd done it on his own terms and escaped to Brighton instead of Edenwhite as his father had so high-handedly commanded. A quick visit to Madame Petra's had secured her company, which had made Cecily happy, as he'd suspected it would.

The Madame had caught wind of the gossip and agreed they must leave London. She also agreed that their time had not yet run its course.

"There is so much more I want to teach you," she'd said while packing her trunk for the trip. "Both of you."

She'd assured him the brothel would be in good hands while she was away, and that a holiday in Brighton would be a welcome one.

The sun had just begun its ascent on the horizon when they'd departed London, just after he had sent a message by footman informing the viscount of their plans. He hated to think that his father had won, but derived a smug sense of satisfaction from his small rebellion. As a man completely dependent on estates he hadn't inherited yet, there were only so many mutinies he could perpetrate before his financial well ran dry. Going to Brighton and taking his and Cecily's mistress with them would be rebellious enough.

He smirked while she entered the room at the thought of her as 'their' mistress. In truth, that's what she was—a woman they had hired to see to both their sexual needs. He almost envied his wife, who'd been privileged to experience Petra in a way he hadn't yet. Though they did have the shared experience of knowing the feel of her skilled mouth. Just the thought of her lips wrapped around his cock caused the organ to swell and fill with blood.

"Are the accommodations to your liking, Petra?"

She closed the door behind her and met him in the center of the room, the firelight outlining her lithe form beneath the sheer fabric she wore.

"Quite comfortable, thank you," she replied. Glancing from him to Cecily and back again, her gaze became observant. "You and your wife do not prepare for bed in the same room, do you?"

He frowned, thinking of the countless nights he'd peered at her through the cracked dressing room door, watching from afar as she loosened and brushed her hair.

"We have separate chambers and dressing rooms," he replied. "Why would we?"

Her laugh—a low, throaty purr—sent even more blood rushing to his cock. God's teeth, this woman had been made for sex. All he could think of was getting her between him and Cecily again.

"It's called intimacy," she replied, striding toward the tub where his wife soaked. "One of the many reasons for your reticence is that you've both been taught that your couplings should be a formal affair, with the husband asking permission from the doorway separating his chamber from the wife's, and her acquiescing. What follows, I suspect, is an encounter during which you hide beneath the covers and rut with the candles blown out. It is a problem I encounter often among couples of the *ton*. You think the formality with which you live your everyday lives must rule your private life, as well."

Kneeling beside the tub, she trailed one finger through the water, swirling it in a slow circle.

He came closer, watching the slender digit slide over Cecily's wet skin. Little droplets of water beaded on her heavy breasts, and the water lapped gently at the tantalizing globes. He held his breath, waiting for Petra to touch her. Yet, she remained coy, tracing a path around the pink circle of her areola, but avoiding the nipple.

Cecily squirmed, opening her eyes. They glittered with desire as they alit on Petra first, then him.

"This goes hand in hand with your lesson on spontaneity," she continued. "Such a simple thing, watching one's wife dress or undress, or bathing ... yet, it opens a level of intimacy that cannot be experienced when you wait on the other side of a door for her to prepare for you."

Truer words had never been spoken. How many times had he fantasized about Cecily at her bath, water sluicing over her decadent breasts, little rivulets running down toward her mound when she stood, trailing down her legs in a sensual, serpentine caress? Experiencing it firsthand made his fantasy pale in comparison.

Coming around behind the tub, he ran his fingers through his wife's hair. Kneeling, he reached for her, tilting her chin up so he could kiss her mouth. She parted her lips for him, answering his questing tongue by greeting it with her own. Moaning, she shifted, causing the water to lap against the sides of the tub.

Opening his eyes, he saw that Petra had taken up a cake of soap.

Rubbing it between her hands, she produced a lather. Putting the cake aside, she slathered Cecily's wet skin with the suds, producing another low moan as her touch skimmed from her shoulders down to her breasts.

"Such a lovely body," she murmured, tweaking the nipples with soapy fingers, then tracing a path over her ribs. "You should experience it in this way. Enjoying your wife's body should not be restricted to intercourse, my lord. A kiss on the neck, a bold caress where no one can see, assisting her in her bath ... all are forms of intimacy that can be performed with no intention of ending in intercourse."

Her lips curved into a smile as Cecily moaned, arching her back and thrusting her breasts upward. His hands joined Petra's, until they both kneaded and massaged Cecily's breasts and ran their soapy hands over her stomach and back up again.

"Of course, if it does end in intercourse ... all the better for you both."

Sheridan followed her lead, taking up the soap and lathering his hands before running it over Cecily's bare skin. Petra moved to the foot of the tub, plucking one of his wife's long legs from the depths of the water. Her hands deftly massaged Cecily's feet and calves before disappearing into the water, moving higher over her thighs. Sheridan concentrated his focus on her upper body, unable to keep his hands from straying back to her breasts at every opportunity.

Pushing her into a seated position, he trailed his hands over her back, tracing the line of her spine down, then back up again to the nape of her neck. Tilting her head back, he wet her masses of golden hair and lathered them, too, smiling when his kneading fingers against her scalp produced another moan of pleasure.

Their ministrations continued until Cecily writhed and moaned between them, not one part of her body going untouched with four hands to tend to her.

Her hips bucked, causing water to splash over the sides of the tub, and he knew Petra's hands teased her mons beneath the surface. She moaned, cheeks flushing pink as she ground her hips against Petra's thrusting fingers.

Reaching back for him, Cecily clawed at the front of his breeches, seeking to free him. His cock pulsed, longing for her touch. Helping her, he freed himself and thrust against her palm. Closing her hand around it, she stroked him boldly, coaxing a bead of moisture from the tip.

His hips moved of their own volition, causing friction between her soft palm and his hard, pulsating shaft. Moaning, he reached for her breasts and cupped them, pinching her erect nipples and pulling a high-pitched cry from deep in her chest. Lips parted, her breath came in short gasps interspersed with moans of pleasure as Petra thrust her fingers rhythmically in and out of her cunt.

He had closed his eyes to give himself over to the moment and the pleasure of it all, when the hot rasp of a tongue caused them to fly open again. Gasping, he gazed down and realized that Cecily's tongue had caressed him, leaving fire in its wake.

His vision blurred and he was taken back to his youth, when a similar act had been performed on him by a whore whose face had been garishly painted. Gritting his teeth, he pulled away from Cecily's hold, avoiding the second flick of her searching tongue.

Brows furrowed, she gave him a questioning glance. Grasping her slender fingers, he wrapped them back around his cock and thrust, showing her what he wanted. Seeming content to follow his lead, she continued stroking him.

A few seconds later, she shuddered, her lips parting on a silent cry as completion carried her away. Petra's fingers slowed, then stilled within her, and she withdrew them, leaning over the tub to plant a kiss on Cecily's lips.

A surge of heat ensued at the sight of the two mouths touching, their tongues caressing between them, and Cecily's hand coming up to squeeze Petra's breast through the fabric of her black peignoir.

His stomach clenched and his bollocks contracted, signaling his climax. Seeming to realize his moment of climax drew near, Petra pulled away from Cecily and moved to kneel before him. Taking the head of his cock into her mouth, she caressed it with her tongue as Cecily continued to fondle him.

A hoarse cry escaped his lips, and he gripped the side of the tub as his knees buckled. His seed filled Petra's mouth in hot spurts, while Cecily continued stroking him, milking him dry.

Releasing him from her mouth, Petra stood. "I do believe this lesson was quite successful."

Yet, somehow, the look in her eyes when she set her gaze on him suggested otherwise. He'd felt her stare on him when he'd pulled away from Cecily's searching tongue, and knew he would have to answer for it later.

For now, however, he had eyes only for his wife, who lay in the tub, more content and relaxed than he'd seen her in ages.

"I shall leave you to your rest now," Petra declared, leaving the room with a swish of her robe. "Until tomorrow morning."

He plucked Cecily from the tub and stood her on shaky legs. He took his time toweling her dry, starting with her hair, then letting his hands and the linen linger on her skin, caressing in slow circles.

"Hmmm," she mumbled when he paused at her breasts, rasping the cloth over her hard nipples. "That feels good."

"Yes?" he prodded.

She nodded. "You're making me want more."

He chuckled, dropping the towel and lifting her. She wrapped her arms around his neck and her legs around his waist while he carried her to the bed.

"You've become insatiable," he murmured, laying her down. Removing all of his clothing, he joined her, covering them both with the counterpane.

"Sherry?" she asked in a voice thick with fatigue.

"Yes, love?"

"Why will you allow Petra to pleasure you with her mouth, but not me?"

His blood ran cold, and tension thrummed through him at her

question. His arms tightened around her, and his pulse raced at the thought of having to answer her.

"Sherry?" she prodded when he didn't answer.

"Oh, that," he replied, forcing a lightness he did not feel into his tone. "It wasn't as bad as all that. Your pretty little fingers just felt so good around my cock, I didn't want you to stop what you were doing."

Giggling, she turned to face him. Her bare skin caressed his, and he decided there was definitely something to be said for sleeping nude with one's wife. His cock sprang to life between them as her hard nipples tickled the hairs sprinkled across his chest.

"I never thought something so simple could drive a man to madness. I hardly did a thing."

Nuzzling her nose with his, he gave her a swift kiss. "Hasn't anyone ever told you the truth about men? We are appallingly simple creatures."

Turning onto her back, she pulled him over her, parting her legs and inviting him into the wet cavern of her core.

"Petra's touch felt nice," she whispered, "but the feel of you inside me is beyond anything I could have ever imagined. I never dreamed I could feel such pleasure. Make love to me, Sherry."

Lowering his lips to hers, he kissed her with a fervor he never had before. Desperation gripped him, and he vowed within himself to do anything to make her happy. If that meant finding some way to purge himself of his father's sadistic measures of educating him, then he would find a way. Perhaps Petra could be of greater help to them than he'd previously thought.

Glad for a distraction for the nonce, he entered his wife in one swift thrust. Moaning, she arched her back and spread her legs wider, sheathing him to the hilt. Losing himself in her, he forgot his troubling memories for a time.

CHAPTER 10

"Tell me about your childhood, my lord."

Cecily tore her gaze away from the passing landscape and gave Petra a quizzical glance. Her request had been anything but —more of a command, really. As a gently-bred woman who'd been taught to defer to men in all things, she had yet to grow used to the other woman's contrary nature. She'd never known a female more self-assured or confident. She'd never seen a woman command everyone around her as if leading puppets on strings. Petra was the sort of woman she wished to be.

Sheridan, who sat on the seat across from them, shifted uncomfortably and cleared his throat. They were alone in the carriage, as James and Cecily's maid followed in a separate conveyance.

"Ah, well ... I suppose it didn't differ much from those of the other lads of the *ton*. I had every comfort in the world, and was cared for by a nanny, then a governess. Of course, then came my years at Eton, then university at Cambridge—"

"Yes, yes," Petra said, a sound much like an annoyed snort cutting between the words. "I am hardly interested in the years you spent being cultivated for life as a viscount. If we are going to discuss your

85

problem, you must delve deeper. I have no concern with the superficial layers that have been wrapped around you to turn Sheridan Cranfield into the Viscount of Perth. Peel them back, and show us the man within. Tell me about your relationship with your father."

He visibly tensed, his jaw grinding and his eyes growing shuttered and guarded. He turned to gaze out the window, avoiding both their gazes.

Cecily frowned, reaching across the vehicle to touch his knee. "Sherry?"

He flinched, then glanced up at her. Her heart broke at the lines of anguish crossing his face. In all the time she'd known her husband, she'd never seen his eyes so shadowed, or his mouth so pinched. The carefree, amiable man she'd married had vanished. Or ... had it all been a façade? Was this the real Sheridan, then? This brooding, sulking man who couldn't even talk about his father?

He placed a hand on top of hers and patted it reassuringly, then cast Petra a dark glare. "I don't wish to speak of him."

Petra nodded. "I suppose not. I suspect he is the crux of your little problem."

"I do not *have* a problem!" he snapped, his voice rising a bit.

Unlike her, Petra did not become ruffled by his sudden shift in mood.

"Of course you do," she insisted, her voice remaining level and calm. "Before your wife hired me, you could only make love to her in one way—in the dark, on top of her, in the most basic and chaste of ways—denying yourself and her the pleasure you both so desperately wanted."

Pursing his lips, he quirked one blond brow. "In the past week, I have licked her cunt, fucked her from behind in a brothel while you looked on, let her ride my cock while she whispered fantasies of the three of us together in my ear, shared her with you on my dining room table, and helped you bathe her body in an inn's bathtub before taking her to bed. I do believe the problem has been solved, to everyone's satisfaction."

Her cheeks heated when he gave voice to every salacious act she had committed with both him and Petra. A slow throb began between her legs, and the memories made her long for more. Yet, it quickly faded as she took in Sheridan's guarded posture.

He hid something, and she wanted to know what.

"You had to be blindfolded in the brothel," Petra pointed out. "You had to be cajoled in the dining room, and last night when Cecily tried to take you into her mouth, you refused her and took me, instead."

"You noticed it, too?" she asked, glancing back and forth between them both. "I ... I thought I had overreacted. He assured me that it was only because ..." she turned back to her husband, her brow furrowing in confusion. "Did you lie to me last night?"

His Adam's apple bobbed when he swallowed. His hands trembled in his lap.

"I don't think—"

"That now is the time?" Petra finished for him. "We have another long day's ride to Brighton and we've only been in this carriage an hour. There is nothing but time."

"Sherry," she said, moving to sit beside him in the carriage. She took his hand and held fast. "I love you. Nothing you tell me about your past will ever change that."

He shook his head. "Yes, it will. I've done things ... you shouldn't have to hear about them."

Exasperation filled her, turning quickly to anger. "Why? Because I'm a delicate porcelain doll to be set on a shelf and admired? I am sick to death of being treated that way! I am a *woman*, Sheridan. I am your wife. Can you not see past your ridiculous notions?"

"You don't understand!" he roared, his face reddening.

She flinched, startled. His expression became contrite, and he took a deep, noisy breath and released it with a sigh.

"Forgive me," he murmured. "It's just that it is not as easy for me to push aside my ridiculous notions, as you call them. They've been ingrained in me since I became old enough to understand the difference between men and women."

She exchanged a glance with Petra, who gave an encouraging nod. "Go on."

"My parents shared a very formal relationship," he began, still avoiding looking at either of them. "They referred to each other as 'my lord' and 'my lady', and never showed affection in front of me and my brother. When I grew old enough to understand intercourse, I often wondered if my parents had only engaged in it twice—just to create Aaron and I—as there existed no evidence that they felt any sort of physical attraction to one another."

"Were they ever affectionate toward you?" Petra asked.

He shook his head. "My father never was. The most he ever did was shake my hand after an accomplishment and say 'well done'. He managed to crack a smile when I completed my education at Cambridge. My mother ... well, I always wondered if she weren't a more affectionate person before she married him. She always seemed to want to show us affection, but he was always there to remind her that it wasn't proper. We were boys, and as such, did not need coddling. He took our rearing in hand. In truth, we hardly ever saw her. Of course, she died when I was twelve, and there never came a chance to truly get to know her."

Cecily's heart dropped into the pit of her stomach at his revelation. What sort of man kept a child from his mother? Of course, a boy needed his father, but he also needed the love of his mother. She did not know her father-in-law well, and realized now it was because Sheridan did everything he could to avoid being anywhere near him. She understood now why he'd been so adamant that they rent their own town residence while in London.

"When I was thirteen, he told me I had become a man," he continued. "He told me I would have urges that were perfectly normal. Men are supposed to explore and slake those urges on any willing female so long as she wasn't a lady. Whores, courtesans, scullery maids ... all fair game."

Petra snorted, rolling her eyes. "Typical."

"When I turned fourteen, he showed me to one of the guest rooms where a young scullery maid waited for me. She was ..." he paused, his cheeks reddening. "Naked. He told me she was my gift and to enjoy her in any way I wished."

Cecily clapped a hand over her mouth. "Dear lord!"

"Did you?" Petra asked, her face still schooled into a mask of calm composure.

He nodded. "I had just turned fourteen and I'd never known a woman before. She had breasts and a cunt, and was willing. Of course I did. I had a bloody good time, too."

The Madame inclined her head, giving him a sympathetic look. "The fun did not last long, did it?"

"No," he confirmed. "This was just the first of many lessons my father taught me about the fairer sex."

"Lessons?" she inquired.

She did not like the turn this conversation had taken, and had a feeling she'd like the rest even less.

"To him, they were as important as the rest of my studies. My conditioning for society and marriage, he said. He wanted to ensure I understood the difference between ladies, and ... well, everything else. He took me to my first brothel when I turned sixteen."

She supposed she didn't conceal the gasp burning in her throat as well as she'd thought, because Petra reached across the carriage to pat her hand reassuringly.

"A common occurrence among men and their sons," she said. "I see it every day."

It would seem she was as delicate and naïve as Sheridan had thought her. She never could have imagined such things took place among London's elite. Oh, of course, she knew men had their vices—drink, gambling, whores—but to take one's young *son* to a brothel seemed a bit uncouth.

"He would allow me to pick the whores, anyone I wanted, but never the same one twice. Because, of course, whores are dispensable and interchangeable. They aren't to be clung to or *cared* about. The first couple of times, he allowed me to go at it alone, and asked me how it went afterward. He was always insistent upon details."

Now Cecily *knew* they'd crossed the line. They no longer spoke of a normal father and son rite of passage. This proved something far more sinister.

"Why did he want details?"

"I did not know, at first," he admitted. "But I knew not to question him. He had his reasons and I always obeyed him. It wasn't until he insisted upon sitting in on my … sessions, that I understood."

Cecily felt as if she would be ill. "He *watched* you?"

"Yes. The first time, I felt so nervous it almost made me ill. He insisted it was necessary and that I would thank him someday. This was an important lesson, one only he could teach me. So, I … I did it. I had intercourse with a whore with him in the same room. Hardly enjoyable for me, though she seemed to have a good time. Of course, she'd been paid to pretend one way or the other. After she left, he descended on me and beat me soundly."

Petra frowned, reacting to this bizarre story for the first time since he'd begun. "Beat you? Whatever for?"

"Apparently, my performance didn't meet his satisfaction. I'd been too nice to her. I'd showed her courtesy. When I thought I'd entered her too roughly, I'd asked if I'd hurt her. When it was over, I gave her towels and a bowl of water to clean herself with. These were my offenses—enough to warrant a facer that nearly knocked me uncon-scious and several blows to the ribs."

"Animal," Petra muttered, her disgust clear.

"On that, we agree," he replied, his tone strained and clipped. "It continued. Each time we went to the brothel, he would watch and tell me what I'd done wrong or right. Then he would instruct me on how a lady must be treated. A man's wife should be a woman above reproach. Pure, chaste, and virtuous. How else could he be certain she would bear him sons that weren't someone else's by-blows? Ladies were delicate, he told me. They didn't have the constitution to stomach a man's voracious attentions."

"But whores could."

He nodded, confirming Petra's statement. "But whores could. Every act other than the most basic practice of penetration, I was taught to perform only on whores or my mistress, if ever I were to take one. If a gently bred girl is taught to close her eyes and think of England when her husband is on top of her, how on Earth is she supposed to react when I ..."

He trailed off, the embarrassed blush coming back to his face.

"Put your cock in her mouth?"

His head snapped up when Petra spoke. The Madame gave him a little smile.

"And here we have arrived at the true reason behind your reticence, my lord," she said. "Your father, with his lessons and beatings, taught you to associate certain sexual acts with whores and women of ill repute. These so-called lessons ... how long did they last?"

"Three years."

Petra sighed. "Long enough to ingrain those foolish notions. It is no wonder you have been holding back."

He ran a shaking hand through his hair and sighed.

"I haven't wanted to," he said, finally looking her in the eye. "You cannot know how hard it's been."

She smiled, reaching up to touch his face. "Yes, I do know. I've wanted more for so long, but I was afraid to speak up, worried you would be disgusted with me."

He laughed, covering her hand with his. "Do you remember our wedding night? I came to you, and you stood there wearing that gossamer bit of white tulle and lace ... Christ, there wasn't an inch of you I couldn't see through the flimsy scrap."

They laughed together, and her heart warmed at the memory.

"How could I forget? I stood there, trembling like a leaf. My mother had told me what would happen; yet, I still felt anxious ... but, I knew you would treat me well."

"I remember picking you up and carrying you over to that bed, and thinking you looked like an angel laying there all in white, on sheets to match, with the moonlight in your hair. I didn't think anything sweeter existed in the world, and I vowed then to protect you from any and everything—including my baser needs. I never wanted to hurt you, and I never wanted to give you reason to look at me and feel disgust."

Wrapping her arms around his neck, she pulled him close for a kiss. He clung to her, accepting her lips and tongue, devouring them as if he'd never tasted anything more satisfying.

"When I look at you, I feel desire," she murmured, pulling away. "It burns deep in my belly, and between my legs, and I know that nothing will satisfy it but you."

He trembled in her arms, his muscles tensing with unreleased strain. She shivered in response, all too aware of the power and virility locked away inside. All that remained was for him to unleash it without restraint.

"Let me be the one you explore your passions with," she whispered. "Let me fulfill your deepest desires."

"I want to," he replied, hands coming up to span her waist. "So very badly. I don't want to hold back from you anymore, but it's so bloody difficult."

"Then we will help you," she said, determination filling her. They'd come so far already; she refused to let up until Sheridan had put his father's grotesque philosophies and teachings behind him. "One step at a time. Isn't that right, Petra?"

She glanced at her ally, and found determination in her eyes, as well.

"We begin right now," Petra declared, a mischievous glint filling her dark eyes.

Sheridan tensed. "Now?"

Petra extended one hand to Cecily. She accepted it, and let the other woman assist her onto the floor of the carriage. Joining her, she knelt and stared up at Sheridan expectantly.

"Yes," she replied, "now. Open your breeches, my lord."

His jaw ticked spasmodically, but curiosity and desire flashed in his eyes.

"Why?" he asked, even as he complied with her wishes.

"I am going to help you associate your sexual desires with your wife. We are going to undo your father's teaching by reconditioning you to see your wife as your sole source of pleasure and desire, no matter how salacious that desire might be."

Sheridan's cock sprang free of his breeches, standing proudly in his lap. Cecily's nipples tightened at the sight, remembering the feel of him inside of her. Yet, there remained one way she hadn't experienced him. Her mouth watered for a taste.

"I am at your disposal," he replied, his voice deep and husky.

She recognized the tones of desire beneath his usual bass.

"Good," Petra replied, smiling. "Your first lesson … allowing your wife the intimacy of taking your cock into her mouth."

His lips parted and his breath hitched. His cock seemed to swell even more in response to her words.

Petra turned to face her. "Would you like that, love?"

She nodded, her own lips parted as the need to fulfill that particular fantasy overcame all else.

"Yes," she replied. "But … I don't know how. Will you teach me?"

The Madame's lips curved into a sensual smile, and she reached up to cup the back of her neck. Petra's lips hovered inches from hers, causing her to tremble with anticipation.

"Nothing would bring me more pleasure," she replied, before capturing her mouth in a fiery kiss.

CHAPTER 11

Sheridan's cock pulsated with need—becoming further exacerbated by the sight of the two beautiful women kneeling before him. He gripped the randy organ, applying pressure to relieve the ache. It hardly aided him, when all he wanted was Cecily's plump lips wrapped around his rod. Or perhaps Petra's. He shivered at the thought of both tongues running up and down his shaft.

His breath hitched, then released on a low groan. The surface of his skin tingled, and he felt as if one touch from either of them would unman him, causing him to finish before they'd even begun.

His throat constricted as he watched them kiss, their writhing tongues meeting between parted lips. Cecily's soft moans filled the carriage, mingling with Petra's low murmurs of satisfaction. Her long, slender fingers gripped the front of his wife's bodice, peeling it down to reveal her breasts. The sweet, pink nipples puckered and hardened when she pinched them, rolling them between her fingers and making Cecily shudder.

Leaning forward, he did the same to Petra, revealing her tits and palming them. Her nipples hardened, rasping his palms as he kneaded the pliant flesh.

Breaking their kiss, Petra turned to him with a cat-like smile.

"The head of a man's cock is quite sensitive," she said, turning back to Cecily. She took his cock in one hand, holding it firmly and causing it to throb in response.

He gasped, thrusting into her hand, desperate for the friction he needed to ease the ache in his groin. She obliged him, giving him a few firm strokes and running her thumb over the slit, drawing a bead of moisture. She smeared it over him, stroking his shaft and teasing his head with her thumb.

His wife looked on, her eyes wide with curiosity as Petra continued stroking him. Leaning forward, she circled him with her tongue, then wrapped her lips around the head and suckled gently.

His hips bucked as he bit back a moan and gripped the carriage seat. He thrust toward her mouth, seeking entrance.

"Ah-ah, my lord," she admonished as she let him go. "It's your wife who desires to take you into her mouth."

She turned to Cecily, using her free hand to give one of her nipples a pinch.

"Don't you, love?"

She nodded, her answer coming out on a breathless sigh. "Yes."

Petra maneuvered herself behind Cecily. Remaining on her knees, she spread her thighs and settled Cecily between them, resting her back against her front. She turned her face inward and planted a kiss on Cecily's jaw.

"Look at your husband," she murmured. "Touch him."

His wife obeyed, reaching out with a tentative hand. Her fingers brushed his shaft, then stroked downward toward his bollocks. He slouched on the carriage seat, leaning back to watch her explore him. After a few more timid touches, she grew bold, wrapping her fingers around his cock the way Petra had done. Her touch branded him, sending a fresh surge of desire through him. If at all possible, his erection swelled even further, eager for more.

"You might be on your knees before him," Petra whispered, reaching up to cup Cecily's breasts from behind. "But your position is one of power. From here, you can command his body. You can claim him in a way you never have before, and bend him to your will. He experiences only the pleasure you choose to give him."

You've bloody well got that right!

Just now, he'd have given Cecily anything she asked, if only she'd wrap those sweet lips around him.

As she stroked him, gently at first, but then with increasing boldness, Petra glanced up and locked gazes with him.

"Look at your wife, my lord," she said. Reaching up, she cupped Cecily's face, tilting it back for better access to her neck. She lowered her head and placed a row of open-mouth kisses along the side of her neck, causing her strokes to slow and her breasts to heave as she shivered in response.

Steadily teasing his wife's nipples, Petra continued, her stare never wavering from his.

"Isn't she beautiful? Such plump, inviting lips." Her thumb stroked along the line of Cecily's jaw, then arced up, caressing her lips.

"Yes," he rasped, his gaze fixated on that thumb as she parted Cecily's lips.

His wife opened her mouth and her pink tongue darted out, stroking the pad of Petra's thumb. His hips surged again and he ground his cock into the tight fist clenching him.

"You want her lips on your hard cock, don't you?" Petra murmured.

"Yes," he repeated.

"Then let her," she insisted. "There is no greater pleasure to be known than between two lovers whose hearts are also engaged. She is your wife. Let her become a vessel for your pleasure, and in turn, you become one for her. She wants this—don't you, my love? Look at your husband and tell him what you want."

Cecily's heavy-lidded eyes met his.

"I want to taste you, Sherry," she said, voice deep and husky with desire. "I want to know the feel of you on my lips, against my tongue. I want to pleasure you with my mouth until you come."

He closed his eyes, trembling at the promise of a fantasy he'd had so many times.

A man's wife must kiss his children with her mouth; it must remain uncorrupted. If you want your cock sucked, find a whore.

The viscount's voice interrupted, sharp and sudden, nearly robbing him of his pleasure. He grit his teeth and opened his eyes, gazing down at the woman on his knees before her. He'd always seen her as an innocent, a prim little English rose who needed his devotion and care. Yet, Petra had peeled back her girlish layers to reveal the woman within. A woman he had always longed to make love to, to experience in every way he could think of.

"Forget what you have been taught," Petra insisted, seeming to sense his drifting thoughts. "If your wife is willing—desiring, even—of this moment, will you deny her?"

He gazed from her to Cecily, his heart gripped by the sight of her wide, pleading eyes. She truly wanted this, wanted him, in a way he'd always dreamed of her wanting him. He would be mad to refuse her.

Pushing the viscount and his grating voice aside, he reached down and took Cecily's hair in a gentle but firm grip.

"No," he answered, pulling her closer.

The head of his cock brushed the seam of her lips, and she parted them. Her darting tongue found the slit of his head and probed it, causing his stomach to clench and his balls to contract. He gasped, his fingers tightening in her hair.

Petra murmured her approval.

"You're a natural," she said to Cecily. "Open your mouth, sweetheart. Let him in."

She obeyed, opening wide to accommodate his girth. He thrust slowly, inching his way into the cavern of her mouth. She brought her tongue up to stroke the underside of his cock, and her mouth closed around him once he'd gone as far as he dared. The urge to push into the back of her throat came at him strong, but he wanted her to become accustomed to the act of fellatio first. For the moment, he concentrated on her, on watching his wife make love to him with her mouth.

"That's it," Petra encouraged, stroking Cecily's hair affectionately. "Take him in and out, just as you would if he were inside your cunt."

She obeyed, pulling back, her cheeks caving as she suckled, then coming forward to envelop him all over again. Her first few attempts felt tentative, a tender exploration. His guttural groans at each pass of her lips over his shaft seemed to embolden her, and before long, she increased her pace, encouraged by his hand leading her through the hair gripped in his fist. His head fell back against the carriage seat and he closed his eyes, losing himself in the fiery sensations she created using only her mouth.

A hand closed around his cock, stroking just beneath Cecily's suckling mouth. He recognized the feel of the slender fingers—Petra. Thrusting against the hand and hot, wet mouth, he moaned, his fingernails digging into the seat cushion as he held on for dear life. As one, they increased their pace even more, driving him closer and closer to the brink.

Swirls of color danced on his closed eyelids as Petra's tongue skimmed the inside of his thigh, before tickling his bollocks.

"Yes," he hissed, his hips moving of their own volition, urging his bulging sack closer to Petra's open mouth.

Her tongue circled them, then her lips drew him in. She suckled while caressing his bollocks with her tongue, increasing his pleasure tenfold.

"Christ, that feels so damn good," he moaned, his voice grown hoarse.

Cecily released his cock from her mouth, joining Petra's tongue with her own.

"Fuck!" he bellowed, feeling inches away from death. Surely, no man could endure pleasure like this and survive it.

Taking his own cock in hand, he stroked, urging himself on toward climax as the two hot, wet mouths caressed and suckled his sac.

"Ah … Christ … I'm going to come," he muttered, his fist tightening as he felt the familiar beginnings of a climax.

Cecily's tongue stroked over the base of his shaft, then scorched a path over his knuckles toward his swollen head. Snatching his hand away, she enveloped him, sucking him until he shuddered and surrendered to release. Thrusting up one last time, he moaned as his seed spurted from him and into her mouth.

Licking her lips, she pulled away and turned her face up to give him a bright smile.

"Come here," he murmured, already reaching down to pull her up into his lap. He set her across his thighs, then wrapped his arms around her and held her tight.

"Thank you," he murmured. "That was …"

"Marvelous," she finished for him. "I quite enjoyed it. Did you?"

He laughed, deftly adjusting the neckline of her bodice, even though he was loathe to cover her lovely tits. The driver would stop soon to change horses, leaving them time for little else. The evening would be soon enough for him to finish what they'd started. He hadn't had nearly enough of her … or their feisty little mistress.

"Darling, if I'd enjoyed any more, I might have died."

She grinned, nestling against his shoulder and closing his eyes. "At least, you would have died happy."

Across from them, Petra had settled back on the seat, every hair and bit of clothing in place. She gave him a smug smirk, her eyes twinkling with promise.

"A lesson well-learned," she declared, folding her hands in her lap. "Well done, my lord. I can hardly wait for the next lesson."

Smiling back at her, Sheridan found he could hardly wait, either.

In the fortnight that followed, Cecily and Sheridan forgot all about the scandal they'd left behind in London. Nothing else mattered here at the seaside, where they experienced a second honeymoon of sorts that proved far more satisfying than the first. Aside from the time spent together, they now had passion and desire to fill their days and nights—a vital component missing from their first wedding trip.

Petra's presence heightened the excitement, and with her help, Sheridan transformed day by day. Gone was the polite, amiable man who used charm as a shield. In his place emerged a confident bloke, simmering with sexuality just beneath the surface. It began to show, making itself plain in the swagger of his walk, the overgrown length of his hair, the rakish scrape of stubble he'd allowed to sprout along his jaw.

How had she never seen him for what he really was? A man of voracious appetite, who never seemed happier than after a good bout of lovemaking? He seemed contented here, freed from the constraints of society and his father's so-called teachings.

Together, she and Petra had purged him of those idiotic notions one by one. When he'd told them that his father had taught him that only whores allowed a man to take a woman while she was on her hands and knees, Petra would hear none of it. She'd reminded him yet again that nothing was forbidden between them, and that if Cecily desired it, he should oblige her. A lesson he was taught again and again—when he took her roughly from behind as he had in the brothel; as he lay her on her back and fucked the cleft between her breasts; as he allowed her to straddle and ride him as he had the night in the library.

Affection came easier to him now, and hardly an hour passed before he would kiss her, touch her, reminding her in the simplest ways that he desired her. A world of pleasure unparalleled became open to her, and Cecily learned she had quite an appetite for sex herself. She grew surprised to discover she enjoyed both Sheridan and Petra equally, and that she would not be averse to continuing their liaison. While she reveled in the time she had with Sheridan alone, nothing could quite compare to the taste of Petra on her tongue as Sheridan fucked her, or the feel of Petra's fingers pumping in and out of her cunt as she sucked her husband's cock. Four hands on her at once, touching, probing, coaxing her to one exquisite ending after the other.

Her husband appeared as attracted to the other woman as she, and before long, the two became allies into seducing her into their bed at every opportunity. The mysterious Madame readily obliged them, fulfilling both their desires with a deftness that never ceased to amaze, despite her reputation.

Their discretion served them well here. The household staff had been told Petra was a cousin of Cecily's accompanying them on holiday. Since they kept their salacious activities confined to the bedroom behind closed doors, no one ever knew what they'd been up to.

She could have remained here forever, with her husband and their lover. Yet, the arrival of an unexpected guest shattered their cocoon of privacy and happiness.

They'd just come from bathing in the ocean when they were apprehended by Hendricks, the seaside house's butler. His grave facial expression betrayed him when he informed them that Sheridan's brother had arrived and asked to see them the moment Sheridan returned.

"It must be important if he came all this way instead of sending a servant," Petra said once he had asked the butler to inform Aaron that they would see him shortly in the drawing room. "I shall give you your privacy."

Leaving them, she departed for the room she'd been given just across the hall from their suites.

As they made their way to their own rooms, Cecily watched her husband with concern.

"What do you suppose he wants?" she asked.

Shaking his head, Sheridan seemed to contemplate her question. His brows furrowed and his mouth became pinched and hard.

"Father likely sent him. Aaron had always been his favorite. It always ate him alive to know I—the one who always despised him and rebelled—would be the one to inherit. I never stopped wondering if they weren't wishing I would fall off my horse or contract pneumonia and die so they could both have their wish, for Aaron to inherit instead of me."

"Do not talk that way," she admonished. "You can hardly blame your brother for being a product of his environment. The viscount made him that way."

He sighed, running a hand through his damp hair. "I suppose you are right. I am no better than he is. For Christ's sake, I couldn't even make love to my wife properly because of him."

Wrapping her arms around him, she stood on tiptoe and gave him a short kiss. "Also something he will have to atone for someday. Do not think of the past any longer, my love. It is behind us. I have never been happier."

He smiled, returning her kiss with a sweet one of his own. "You're right, I suppose."

"Shall we dress and meet him together?"

Pulling away from her, he shook his head. "Let me find out what he wants on my own. You ring for a bath and take the afternoon for yourself. Rest. Or..." he grinned, reaching up to find her breast and give it a gentle squeeze. "Go see what Petra's up to. I am certain she can keep you occupied."

She giggled. "You naughty boy! Have we not caused enough scandal?"

He arched one brow and gave her a wicked grin. "You cannot possibly know how mad it will drive me to think of what the two of you are doing up here while I'm down there dealing with him."

Her hips swayed beneath her white, cambric bathing dress as she turned to retreat to her chamber.

"I hope it drives you mad with longing," she said before disappearing into her dressing room.

His laughter followed her, causing warmth to blossom in her chest. She didn't think she'd ever heard him laugh—truly laugh because he was amused. It thrummed like a different sort of laugh, not the one he used in public out of courtesy when someone told a dry joke.

As she rang for her maid and began removing her wet bathing

clothes, she found herself hoping it would last. Aaron's visit did not have to change anything. The moment Sheridan got rid of him, they could go back to being blissfully happy.

She slid into her dressing gown just as her maid entered. After requesting a bath and pot of hot chocolate, she relaxed before the fire while she waited. She half-expected Sheridan to return right after going down to greet Aaron and tell her they'd been worried for nothing. Perhaps he'd come to tell them some new scandal had overshadowed theirs and that it was safe to return to London again.

Yet, as she lingered in the bath, washing her hair and soaking, the minutes ticked by. She left the tub and tucked herself into her dressing gown again while her maid brushed her hair before the fire, indulging in two cups of the steaming chocolate. Still, he did not come.

Something was wrong.

The uneasiness grew and settled into the pit of her stomach, until she thought the chocolate might make a reappearance. She began to grow worried and dismissed her maid, even though the time to dress for dinner fast approached.

When he finally returned, she ceased her pacing before the hearth and rushed forward to meet him.

"Sherry!" she exclaimed when her gaze settled on his haggard face.

His eyes were vacant, almost unseeing, his brow furrowed as if some heavy burden rested upon his shoulders.

"What is it?" she asked when he didn't speak. "Has something happened in London? Why did he come?"

His gaze finally met hers, as if he'd just realized she occupied the room.

"It's my father," he said, his voice a strangled whisper. "He's dead."

CHAPTER 12

Sheridan faintly registered his wife and her ministrations. She flitted about him with the concern of a crooning mother, bringing him tea, soothing his brow with gentle fingers, and giving him time to recover from the shock Aaron had delivered barely an hour ago.

Though a short time had passed since his brother had arrived with the news, he felt as if he'd been sitting there for a fortnight—staring off into space with Cecily fussing over him.

He reached out, grasping one hand a bit roughly, causing her steps to falter. She'd been going to ring for something, though he didn't know what. Food, most likely. His sweet dove of a wife always seemed to think someone needed tea and cakes at a time like this. Never mind the fact that he could barely swallow past the fist-sized lump lodged in his throat.

She glanced down at him, her brow creased in concern, her lower lips trembling. Sighing, he pulled her forward, between his spread legs, and grasped her waist tightly. Leaning forward, he rested his forehead against her abdomen, inhaling her familiar scent. Her hands came up to slide through his hair, her fingers deftly removing the fastening James had used to hold it back. She stroked the locks affectionately, waiting silently for him to speak.

What could he say?

He'd gone downstairs with that smug smile still on his face and fantasies of him with Petra and Cecily running through his mind. Even seeing his brother's stoic expression hadn't taken the wind out of his sails. Aaron had always been a stodgy sort.

It wasn't until his brother spoke that he understood.

Aaron had stood from the chair he'd been lounging in, having tea while waiting for him to appear, and inclined his head.

"My lord," he'd said.

Those two words had doused him like a bucket of ice water.

While Petra and others of the merchant and lower classes referred to all peers of the realm as 'my lord' or 'my lady', Sheridan was never addressed as such by those in the *ton*. He had only been the son of a viscount, a gentleman, but without a title; wealthy, but landless. It had always been Mr. Cranfield.

Always.

Aaron would always have called him 'Sheridan', never 'my lord'. It had been his way of informing him that he had inherited. He hadn't missed the spite with which his brother addressed him. The second son of the viscount had always been envious of his position.

He had taken a moment to recover as a hundred emotions had assailed him at once. Once the shock wore away, a sense of panic settled in. He hadn't thought to become the Viscount for another ten years, at least. His father was no old bloke. He'd always been healthy as a horse, active in riding and fencing. He'd never been sick a day in his life—at least, Sheridan could never remember such a time.

Once the panic over whether he felt ready to take over the viscountcy faded—honestly, he'd been preparing for it his entire life— indifference settled in. He'd hated Baldwin with a passion. No matter how hard he tried, Sheridan couldn't muster a single ounce of sadness over the man's death.

He'd cleared his throat and strode to the sideboard, foregoing tea for a splash of brandy.

"When?" he asked, swishing the amber liquid around his tumbler and avoiding his brother's gaze. "How?"

"Three days ago," Aaron replied. "As to how ..."

His pause caught Sheridan's attention, and he glanced up from his brandy. His gaze locked with his brother's, and he realized then that there had been a reason he'd come instead of a servant. Something horrible had happened and only a family member could be trusted to relay the news.

He took the brandy in one swallow and refilled the glass, pouring one for Aaron, as well. Despite their differences, they were brothers. The man obviously felt something akin to grief for their father.

Placing the glass in Aaron's hand, he reached out and gave his brother's shoulder a pat.

"Take your time," he encouraged, before downing another sip of his own drink. "Tell me what happened."

Aaron's hand shook as he finished the brandy in two quick swallows, wincing as it went down.

"It is a good thing Father discouraged eavesdropping amongst the servants," he muttered. "We do not have to worry that what I'm about to say will leave this room."

A niggling of dread tickled the back of his neck. If Aaron didn't want servants overhearing, it must be awful.

"Well?"

Aaron took a deep breath and sighed, setting his empty glass aside. Placing the trembling hand in his pocket, he carried on.

"His valet found him, seated before the fire ... with a bullet lodged in one temple."

Sheridan started, his heart thudding in his chest. "I beg your pardon?"

"He held the gun in his hand," he whispered.

He shook his head in disbelief. "It makes no sense. The viscount would never—"

"*You* are the viscount now," Aaron reminded him. "And I know, he would never have *murdered* himself. I do not believe it for a moment."

Sheridan gasped. "You don't mean ... someone else?"

He nodded. "I believe I know who, but I cannot prove it."

"Who?"

His brother stepped closer, lowering his voice even more, so that Sheridan barely heard him.

"Jeanette."

He laughed, thinking of their meek, quiet stepmother. "You must be joking."

"Our father's murder is no laughing matter," Aaron insisted.

"Of course not," he agreed. "But your assertion that it could have been Jeanette is. Come now, Aaron. You know the woman is as meek as a mouse. It's why he chose her. Yet another person he could grind under his thumb. The poor thing is probably numb from shock—I do hope you didn't level your ridiculous accusations at her."

His brother straightened, raising his chin a notch. "Of course not. As I said, I have no proof. However, the pistol was found in his left hand, and the bullet went through the left temple."

He nodded in understanding. "Ah, I see. Father was right-handed."

"Precisely."

He ran his hands through his hair again, giving it a slight tug. The pain did not wake him, so he had to assume this wasn't some sort of dream.

"Who knows about the manner of his death? Please tell me you did not alert the authorities."

"Of course not! Do you think me daft? If it is thought he killed himself, his legacy will be ruined!"

He scoffed. "I do not give a bloody damn about his fucking legacy."

Aaron sniffed, curling his nostrils as if offended by his crude language. "You should, as that legacy now belongs to you. We would be ruined."

"Who knows, Aaron?"

"Jeanette, of course, and Yearly, his valet."

Sheridan nodded. "Good. Let's keep it that way. As you said, we'd be ruined."

"That *woman* would be the ruined one if she were exposed as the murderer. The *ton* would have nothing but pity for us."

"You will do nothing regarding our stepmother," Sheridan commanded.

For once, Aaron had no choice but to listen. Sheridan had become the Viscount of Perth, which meant he now controlled every aspect of his brother's life, including his finances. "The woman is a widow now, and we will give her the respect she is due."

His brother looked as if he wished to protest, but wisely refrained.

"Where is his body?" he asked.

"On its way to Edenwhite," he replied. "We put about a false story— a carriage accident that left him severely disfigured. We have allowed no one to see the body."

He nodded. "A wise decision. We will leave for Edenwhite at dawn and see him buried. I will send for Jeanette. It will fall to me to see her compensated for her years of ill-treatment."

Aaron scoffed. "Oh, cry off, Sheridan. He never gave her anything she didn't deserve."

"And our mother? What did she deserve?"

He avoided Sheridan's stare, the green gaze identical to his own wandering to the carpet. He could not pretend ignorance concerning the beatings. Apparently, his sons weren't the only ones the viscount liked to punish physically.

"When will you face the truth about him? The man was a monster whose sole intent was to control every aspect of our lives. He is gone now and we are free. Aren't you relieved?"

Aaron shook his head. "He was a man, which is more than I can say for you."

"I see. His teachings took root in you. He's done to you what he failed to do to me—he's turned you into him. I pity you, brother."

He ignored Sheridan's statement, turning to exit the drawing room. "I shall take my customary chambers. Do not expect me for dinner."

Sheridan came back to the present now—to the soothing touch of his wife and the comfort of her nearness and scent. Glancing up at her, he took a deep breath.

"I'm sorry, my love. Our time of respite is over. We leave for Edenwhite in the morning."

The journey to Edenwhite proved long and relentless. Adding to the tedium of the arduous trip, Cecily had been forced to endure riding with her lady's maid—whose company could be likened to that of a piece of wood. Petra had been sent back to London in the carriage the maid and Sheridan's valet had occupied on the way to Brighton. It hadn't seemed appropriate to bring her to Edenwhite, under the circumstances.

"It's not as if anyone cares he's gone," she muttered, bitterness curling her upper lip.

Damn the man—he'd gone and died and spoiled her time away from London with the two people she cared most about.

"I beg your pardon, my lady?" her maid said, glancing up from her knitting needles. Her mousy brown hair hung limp on either side of her round, plain face.

Cecily sighed—she was no Petra.

"Nothing, Abby," she murmured, turning to gaze through the carriage window.

Sheridan, James, and Aaron rode on horseback, leaving her without even her husband for company.

All she had were her thoughts, which had become one confusing muddle, causing a dull throb to pulse between her eyes.

What would happen now that he had inherited? Sheridan Cranfield, Viscount of Perth, had a beautiful ring to it. Not just because of the wealth and land that came along with it, but because her husband had just become considerably more influential. That power could be enough to gloss over the little mess they'd left behind in London—especially when coupled with the death of his father and ascension to the title.

Of course, that was assuming they could continue to keep the manner of the previous viscount's death a secret.

They would likely spend the season at Edenwhite, as returning while in mourning would be inappropriate. Besides, Sheridan had duties to fulfil as the new Viscount and much to do to acclimate himself to the new position.

By this time next year, the *ton* would have forgotten about her little indiscretion. Perhaps her friends would even allow her to rejoin her charity groups. If not, well, she had become a viscountess with the wealth and means to begin her own organization.

Perhaps when they returned to London, it would be with a babe in tow.

The thought caused a small smile to curve the corner of her mouth. A babe was a possibility she'd known to be inevitable, but one she hadn't given much thought to until now.

With their intimate life made right, trying to make an heir would become far more enjoyable. She looked forward to the day she could tell Sheridan she carried their child.

She spent the rest of the day daydreaming about babies and nurseries—as thoughts of Petra, Sheridan, and the passion they'd shared together in London and Brighton would only cause her to become aroused. There would be time enough for that once they'd arrived at Edenwhite.

She couldn't pretend not to be disappointed that their time with the sultry Madame had ended. There remained so much they'd yet to experience together.

By the time they reached the estate, her melancholy had returned. The sky had turned overcast, hinting at a coming storm. All around them, Edenwhite had fallen into an odd sort of stillness, as if all of its inhabitants felt oppressed by the looming cloud of death.

The servants awaiting them on the front steps of the manor made a somber portrait—dressed all in black with the gray sky hanging overhead. Cecily tried to ignore them and study her new home as Sheridan handed her down from the carriage.

She craned her neck, taking in the smooth, white pillars and looming front doors. The manor looked quite different now than it had during the winter. Green ivy climbed the house's façade, and the neatly-manicured lawns would look quite beautiful when the sun shone. Smiling, she turned her gaze up to meet his from beneath the brim of her hat.

She maintained her smile and polite demeanor while she was introduced to each member of the household staff. By the time they were ushered into the house with promises of a light supper, her feet ached and her face hurt from smiling so much. Yet, it seemed a small price to pay to put the staff at ease. She did not know what sort of mistress the previous viscountess had been, but Cecily had always been easy to please.

As they stood in the main hall being relieved of their coats and hats, the butler, Bosworth, approached them and cleared his throat.

"My lord, my lady, a visitor awaits you in the garnet drawing room."

Sheridan scowled. "A visitor? With my family in mourning and us only just arrived? Whoever it is, send them away. We are not taking callers today."

The butler cleared his throat again. "I am afraid the visitor has taken up residence in one of the guest rooms. We felt obligated to allow it until you arrived, my lord."

It became Cecily's turn to frown. "You would not happen to refer to the dowager viscountess, would you?"

Bosworth inclined his head. "Indeed, my lady."

"For God's sake, man!" Sheridan thundered, brushing past him and heading toward said drawing room. "The dowager is hardly a guest in her own home. Of course she can remain. In fact, I want the dower house prepared for her immediately. It is hers, as promised in her marriage settlement agreed upon by my father. I intend to uphold that promise."

The butler indicated no feeling on the matter one way or another. With a stiff bow, he departed to carry out the viscount's instructions.

Aaron's face twisted into a mask of revulsion, as if detecting an offending odor. "I will not suffer her presence, Sheridan," he declared. "I can hardly be expected to dine at the same table with her."

"Then you'd best get on the road to the village before the sky begins to darken," her husband said without turning around. "I am certain there are plenty of warm, dry rooms, and a fine meal there you can take by yourself."

Cecily turned away from her brother-in-law's reddening countenance and hurried after Sheridan, who had paused before the door to the garnet drawing room—so named because of its rich, red décor. She pressed a hand to the small of his back and gave him an encouraging nudge.

"Would you like some privacy?" she offered.

She understood that despite his hatred for his father, Sheridan might have mixed feelings about facing a woman who stood accused of murdering him. If he felt anything like Cecily did, he might be torn between hugging her tight while thanking her, or pretending not to know the truth ... or rather, what might be the truth. No confession had been forthcoming.

He turned, wrapping an arm around her and kissing the crown of her head. "I'd like you to come in, too, if it's not too much trouble. Perhaps she'll be more at ease with another woman in the room."

"Whatever you need," she replied.

He opened the door to reveal his stepmother, seated in an armchair near the fire. She appeared quite gothic in her dark, red surroundings, shrouded in unrelenting black. Her porcelain complexion had gone ashen, her dark brown eyes dull and lifeless. Her dark hair had been pulled back into a simple chignon, without even a single strand left free to soften her features.

Yet, even dressed as a widow, the dowager viscountess appeared little more than a child. Cecily recalled that she and her stepmother-in-law were of an age.

She stood as they approached and curtsied, keeping her eyes lowered to the carpet.

"My lord," she murmured. "Welcome home."

"Hello, Jeanette," he replied, forcing a smile. "You look well."

She scoffed, resuming her seat in the chair. "Nonsense. I look ghastly. I only arrived this morning, just ahead of you."

"I have ordered the dower house prepared for you," he said, coming straight to the heart of the matter.

Jeanette smiled, transforming her face and reminding them of the radiant beauty she'd once been. Before marriage to the viscount had turned her into the meek, mousy thing seated before them.

"That is kind of you."

Sheridan shrugged. "It is no more than you are owed. As well, what remains of your dowry will be released to you—use it as you please. In addition, I hope you will allow me to provide a stipend for you. I wish to see you well taken care of."

Her eyebrows shot up. "Do you? Why, I wonder?"

His brow creased. "It is my duty as the new viscount to see to your well-being. Consider it ... a form of compensation for ..."

"For the years I bore your father's cruelty?" she finished, pursing her lips.

He sighed, running a hand through his hair. "There is nothing I can do to compensate you for that. However, I hope to make the rest of your life comfortable."

Jeanette fell silent for a moment, her gaze becoming unfocused. Sheridan glanced at her, seemingly concerned and uncertain how to proceed. Cecily cleared her throat.

"Jeanette, you seem distressed," she said, keeping her voice low and even. As things stood, the woman looked as if a slightly raised voice might send her into a fit of tears. "Perhaps it will help to talk about whatever it is that's bothering you. We are still family, after all. His lordship and I want to help you in any way we can."

The widow laughed aloud, seeming genuinely amused. "Help me? I suppose you feel obligated to try. No need, my dear. If there is one thing being married to Baldwin taught me, it was how to take care of myself."

"Yes," she replied. "I can see you are quite a resourceful woman."

"We quarreled that night, you know," she said.

Cecily nodded encouragingly. "That happens in a marriage. Sheridan and I quarrel often."

A bald-faced lie. They hadn't been married long enough to fight, and had spent much of the last few weeks sharing a female lover. However, Jeanette did not need to know that. She seemed on the verge of a confession and Cecily did not want to ruin that.

"It was awful," Jeanette continued, as if she hadn't spoken. "I had bought a new ballgown and thought to surprise him. It was a lovely thing—periwinkle with cream lace and pearl adornments."

She smiled. "It sounds quite lovely."

Jeanette frowned. "When I met him in the front hall, to leave for the Amerson's annual fête—he told me I looked like a whore."

Sheridan drew in a sharp breath. Her heart ached for the poor thing. She had been too young, too beautiful, and too sweet to endure a man like Baldwin Cranfield.

"I am certain he didn't mean it," Cecily soothed, even as she knew the words were a lie.

Jeanette snorted. "Of course he did. It was quite decadent—with quite a low neckline. I just thought ..." She trailed off and sighed.

"You wanted to look beautiful for him," Cecily supplied. "There is nothing wrong with that."

She shrugged. "I suppose I thought if he were pleased with my appearance, perhaps ... oh, it was so silly! I'd hoped he would be pleased enough to treat me well, for a change. Even just one night. I'd grown so tired ..."

Sheridan nodded. "A sentiment I well understand. He was an impossible man to please."

"As he proved that night," she said. "He took my arm and dragged me upstairs to my chambers, where he proceeded to question me about who I had dressed to please." She paused, laughing out loud and grasping her stomach. "He accused me of having a lover—as if I were ever allowed to go anywhere without him or one of his footmen dogging my every step. It did not matter what I said—he would not believe me. He told me if he could not pry the truth from me, perhaps …"

Her husband's shoulders tensed, his neck cording, the vital vein beneath this skin throbbing.

"He would beat it out of you," he whispered.

She nodded, lowering her eyes. A tear fell onto the back of her hand. "When it was over, he left me lying in bed, crying. He'd torn the sleeve of my dress and ripped the pearls along the bodice loose. I so loved that gown."

Cecily leaned forward, perched on the edge of her chair and in danger of falling on her arse on the floor at any moment. Sheridan seemed to hold his breath, as well, while they both waited for her confession to come.

Jeanette sniffled and raised her head. Tears streaked her face, her nose and cheeks stained red.

"I must have lain there for hours, crying. I believe I fell asleep—honestly, I cannot remember. I can only recall closing my eyes for a moment, and awakening to the sound of screams. A chambermaid had discovered his body in the library. On his desk sat an empty bottle of port. In his hand, a revolver. The room still reeked of gunpowder and blood when I arrived to find him dead."

Sheridan leaned forward, resting his elbows upon his knees. "The gun was in his hand, yes?"

She nodded. "Yes. I cannot fathom what drove him to do it, Sherry. Your father had always been a prideful man. I never would have dreamed he would take his own life."

Cecily watched them both—the sniffling Jeanette, and her pensive husband. She digested the widow's words, turning them over in her mind and searching for any hidden meaning she might have missed.

"Jeanette," he said, his voice low. "I am certain you know that my father was partial to his right hand."

A small sound, akin to a gasp, escaped her. Cecily would have missed it if she'd dared to breathe. Jeanette's gaze flitted away for a moment, then came back to Sheridan.

"Of course."

His jaw ticked. "The pistol was found in his left hand. Odd, that."

She raised her chin a notch, her nostrils flaring. "Your father was a man of many ... eccentricities. As I am sure you are aware."

His jaw tightened, and his folded hands gripped each other tight.

"Yes, he was. Still, one cannot help but wonder ..." He trailed off, giving her a pointed look. "If you knew of someone who wished him ill, you would tell me, wouldn't you?"

Jeanette chuckled, appearing delirious even in the midst of her grief. "Would I, my lord? Should I?"

"You owe him nothing," he agreed. "Nor are you indebted to me in any way. But I ... I need to know."

Her eyes darted as she seemed to search her mind for any shred of truth. Cecily wondered if the woman would share it with them, even if she found it.

"Your father was a powerful man," she whispered. "He had no enemies that I knew of. Besides, no one was at home but us."

"What of the household staff?" Cecily asked. "Perhaps a servant with a grudge?"

She shook her head. "Our staff are loyal. They would never go against him. Oh, there were a few who indulged me behind his back. I suppose they felt sorry for me. They might have looked the other way while I spent more than I was allowed, or flirted a bit. I am so grateful to them all."

Sheridan sighed, running a hand over his haggard face. "Forgive me. This is has all been so ..."

"Arbitrary?" Jeanette said. "Outlandish? I could not have written a greater farce for the stage if I'd tried."

"Forgive us," Cecily cut in, placing a hand on her husband's arm. "I am certain you're exhausted after your journey. We did not mean to turn this into an interrogation."

Sheridan looked tense, but did not contradict her. "Her Ladyship is right; of course, we do not mean to interrogate you. This has been a shocking event, and we are all a bit surprised and tired after such a long journey. Will you join us for dinner?"

Jeanette stood. "Thank you, but I believe I'll turn in early tonight. I would love to take breakfast with you in the morning, however."

Sheridan stood and extended a hand to her. "We would enjoy that, thank you."

She placed her hand in his, and he bent to kiss it. Jeanette breezed past him to find Cecily in her path. She paused, gazing up at her expectantly.

Cecily reached out and took her hands, gripping them tightly. "I hope if you need anything, you will come to me. I know that you are my stepmother-in-law, but we are of an age. I am here for you, whatever you need."

Jeanette became teary again, gripping her hands tight. "Thank you. You are a good woman. A fine wife for my stepson."

She reached out and pulled the other woman into an embrace.

"Let me help you," she whispered, her voice so low, only Jeanette could hear her. "Tell me which servant killed for you. I know you did not do it, but … the circumstances …"

Jeanette's fingers dug into her back and she held fast. "Peter," she whispered. "A footman. He always pitied me because of Baldwin's rough treatment. We were not lovers, but … I think we might have wanted to be."

Pulling away, Cecily gave her a nod. Composing herself quickly, she smiled.

"Rest well."

Jeanette curtsied to them both. "Good night."

After she had left, her husband turned to her.

"What on Earth was that about?" he asked. "A more bizarre moment, I couldn't have imagined."

She laughed. "It only seemed bizarre because you aren't a woman. Everything she said seemed perfectly clear to me."

With a smirk, he wrapped his arms around her, drawing her against his body. "Care to enlighten me?"

Taking his face in her hands, she stared deep into his eyes.

"She didn't kill him," she whispered. "Her lover did. Or, rather, the man who loves her did."

He sighed, as if in relief, sinking into her. "That is all I wanted to know. I don't give a damn about the bastard, and I'm certain she does not, either. His death is the best thing that could have happened to us both."

"I know, and now it's over."

"I only wish I knew how to reward her," he replied. "She, or her amour, have performed what I like to think of as a civic duty."

She grinned. "There is a footman named Peter living at Perth House. I think it would be nice if he were relocated to Edenwhite. I do believe the dower house is understaffed. He would do nicely to round out the household."

His eyes widened, and his mouth fell open. Then, he smiled, and chuckled.

"You, my love, are a wonder. Not just beautiful and passionate, but sharp as a nail. Have I told you lately how much I adore you?"

Reaching up to grasp her bodice, she jerked it down, exposing her breasts. Her nipples hardened at the sharp gasp that escaped his throat, caused by the sight of her bare tits. He ground his hips into hers, pressing his hard cock against her soft mound.

"Perhaps you should show me," she murmured. "Right here, right now."

Lifting her until she wrapped her legs around his waist, he strode toward the nearest couch.

CHAPTER 13

NINE MONTHS LATER ...

Sheridan Cranfield, Viscount of Perth, stepped from the confines of Brooks' and into the dark, snowy night. Inhaling, he purged his nostrils of the stench of stale cigars and brandy, filling it with the fresh, clean scent of winter. His lungs burned from the cold, but he embraced it. Swinging his walking stick, he set off toward home, glad he'd decided against bringing a carriage.

The old Sheridan might have ridden in a carriage. He might have remained late into the night with his friends, who would have once made him feel obligated to stay. All in the name of amity.

Amiable. Selfless. Predictable.

Those attributes might have described Mr. Cranfield in the past, but the Viscount of Perth had become a new man. Gone was the voice of his father dictating his every decision. The weight bearing down upon him and reminding him of his past had been lifted, and with his father's death had come a freedom unlike anything he'd ever known.

He almost felt tempted to skip along the path, kicking up snow in his wake.

The mask had been pulled away and the gentle chap who had always sought to present a false veneer to the world had been banished. In his place stood the man Sheridan had always wanted to be—self-assured, confident, and independent.

Spending the season at Edenwhite had proved a wise course of action. It had given them time and distance away from London, and his transition into the role of viscount had been a seamless one. His stepmother-in-law had been settled happily into the dower house. She hardly ever emerged from the little dwelling, but when she did, he'd noticed her improved appearance each time. Week by week, her complexion grew rosier, her figure fuller and healthier, her smile a bit wider. He supposed the hiring of a footman named Peter had gone a long way toward soothing her grief. Apparently, the death of his father had lifted more than just his own burdens.

Aside from giving him time to adjust to the title, their reprieve in the country had also meant more time spent with Cecily. Of course, he'd had to find time with her when their schedules permitted. His wife had taken to the role of viscountess with the aplomb he'd known she possessed. Her skill at organization and her charitable heart had turned her into the darling of Edenwhite and its people. They always seemed happy to see her when she went to visit them, inquiring about their needs and bringing necessary supplies. Every time she struck out on a journey over the estate, she returned with a basket laden with baked goods and hand-made gifts from their tenants. They adored her, almost as much as he did.

The passion that had been ignited in her during their time with Petra had persisted—not snuffing out, but growing like a roaring fire. Their nights, and many of their free afternoons, had been spent in ardent attempts at producing an heir. He had never felt anxious about the matter of children, knowing they would come when the time was right. In the meantime, they'd had a rollicking good time trying to sire one.

Finally, during their last weeks in the country, she'd confessed to having gone several weeks without her courses. She hadn't wanted to be premature, but felt fairly certain that they would have a son or daughter by summer.

Christmas in London with his pregnant wife. He could think of nothing sweeter.

The *ton*, as predicted, had latched onto some new bit of scandal and forgotten all about Cecily's supposed indiscretion. While a few of the more pious sorts still avoided her, the majority of their peers had welcomed their return, many visiting to offer their condolences for the death of his father.

All was as it should have been, and he supposed he owed it all to the two women who had turned his life upside down. Smirking, he allowed his thoughts to wander to Petra as he wondered how she'd spent the season. He couldn't deny that his thoughts strayed to her occasionally, especially since her time with them had ended so abruptly. If nothing else, he ought to visit her sometime, just to thank her for what she'd done for him and Cecily.

"I say, Cranfield ... is that you?"

He paused in his steps, head drawn up sharply by the familiar voice. A deep baritone with just a hint of arrogance behind it. A voice that had once caused him revulsion.

However, as he glanced up into the gaze of Camden Rycroft, His Grace the Duke of Avonleah, he felt none of the bitterness he might have expected to feel when coming face to face with the man who'd stolen a woman right out from under him. He felt no resounding ache he ought to have felt, seeing him with Margaret on his arm, or noticing the rather large belly pressed against the front of her redingote.

"Ah, but it is Perth now, darling," Margaret reminded him.

"Yes, quite right. Forgive me, Perth."

His smile felt genuine as he bowed to the duke, then curtsied to his duchess.

"Avonleah, Duchess," he said, inclining his head. "How lovely to see you. Out for an evening stroll?"

"Margaret's grown a bit restless trapped inside the house," Camden replied, giving her an affectionate look.

He might have thought the man a pretentious snob at one time, but no man could deny that he was smitten with his wife.

"You would be, too, if you were married to an overbearing duke who didn't allow you to step beyond your front door," she quipped back.

"Now, now, my dear," he crooned. "No upsets. It isn't good for the babe."

Sheridan cleared his throat. "Congratulations, by the way. Your first child—that is splendid news."

Margaret smiled. "Oh, but we have just heard that the viscountess is expecting, as well."

"Yes, though she's much earlier in her confinement than you."

She rolled her eyes and scoffed. "Confinement, bah! As if carrying a child is cause for locking a woman away for nine miserable months."

"It is," Avonleah said. "At any rate, we shan't hold you up, Perth. I am certain you're anxious to get home to your wife."

That he was.

He bowed again. "Enjoy your evening."

As he walked past them, Margaret reached out and gently touched his arm. He paused, gazing down at the woman he'd once thought himself in love with.

There was no denying her beauty. Apricot skin, sable locks, and velvety brown eyes. Becoming a wife and mother had changed her, making her more womanly than the girlish thing she'd been just last year. Yet, he could conjure no feelings for her beyond those of amiable friendship. Odd, that. He'd once thought he'd never recover from the pain of losing her to someone else.

Perhaps, then, he'd never loved her as much as he'd supposed. After all, he'd thought her the epitome of what his viscountess should be—

innocent, sweet, with a spotless reputation. The sort of woman his father would have wanted for him. Which wasn't to say that, perhaps, he couldn't have found passion with her. Yet, when he thought of nights spent in bed with the woman he loved, the only face he saw was Cecily's.

"You seem so different, Sheridan," she murmured. Then she smiled. "You seem happier. Yes, that's it. Are you happy?"

He smiled down at her, remembering the day she'd turned down his proposal and accepted Avonleah's, instead. She'd fixed that wide stare on him then and asked him to try to find happiness.

Patting her hand, he nodded. "Happier than I ever thought I could be. I suppose I have you to thank for that."

Avonleah cleared his throat. "Hello? Rakish, fiancée-stealing duke standing right here. Don't I get any credit?"

Sheridan laughed. "Very well. Thank you."

"You're quite welcome," she replied, giving his arm another squeeze, then letting go. "Merry Christmas, Sherry."

"Merry Christmas to you both," he replied before continuing on his way.

Lowering his head against the cold, he quickened his pace.

He arrived home to find that the house had gone quiet for the night. It had grown rather late, and while he might usually find Cecily reading in the library, waiting up for him, he knew her delicate condition often tired her. She had taken to going to bed earlier and sleeping later.

Taking the stairs two at a time, mind filled with thoughts of awakening her by crawling beneath the sheets and placing his head between her legs, he quickly found his way to their suite of rooms. Dismissing James, he made quick work of undressing for bed.

Wearing nothing beneath his robe, he crossed through his dressing room and hers, hoping his wife would be up for a bit of bed play. He did not wish to tire her, but since she'd announced her pregnancy, she'd become even more irresistible to him.

His breath caught in his throat and his mouth went dry as he paused on the threshold, greeted by the sight he'd least expected.

Cecily did not sleep—she waited for him, draped across the bed wearing a thin wisp of red material. He supposed it might have been called a nightgown if it weren't so indecent. Her breasts—made even fuller by pregnancy—spilled from the front, and thin, almost non-existent straps held the thing up over her shoulders. A slit in the gown's skirt bared one creamy thigh.

A vixen wearing a similar getup in black lay beside her. Long, lithe limbs and taut, high breasts were as tantalizing as his wife's display of creamy flesh. Dusky skin and dark hair made a startling contrast against Cecily's blonde hair and fair skin.

His wife sat up and crawled to the edge of the bed. "Welcome home, my love."

With a grin, he came farther into the room, watching as his wife unfolded her long, shapely legs and stood.

"Welcome home, indeed," he chuckled. "To what do I owe this pleasant surprise?"

"Think of it as an early Christmas gift," she replied. "Are you pleased?"

He raised his eyebrows. "Two beautiful women waiting for me in my bed? Pleased doesn't quite seem to fit the moment."

She smiled, extending one hand to Petra and helping her from the bed. The dark-haired beauty reached up, inching her fingers beneath the straps of her gown. She pulled and they snapped, falling away. The gown slithered down to her waist, hanging from her hips and baring her breasts and belly.

Cecily circled behind her, pressing her body against the other woman's from behind. Her hand slipped around Petra's waist and down into the confines of the gown hanging from her hips. Sheridan's cock leapt to attention at the sight of Cecily's hand disappearing between her legs, concealed by the fabric.

She turned to place a kiss along Petra's jaw, working her way down to her shoulder, her opposite hand coming up to cup one firm breast. Petra moaned, allowing her head to fall back against Cecily's shoulder as Cecily teased her nipple and cunt simultaneously.

Sheridan reached for the belt of his dressing gown, loosened it, and allowed it to fall to the floor. Primal satisfaction filled him as both women fixed their gaze on him, and two pairs of eyes began tracing the bulges and sinews of his nude body.

"As a reward for completing your sessions with me," Petra said as Cecily continued to fondle and tease her, "this final session will become about you and your desires. Cecily and I are at your disposal, my lord. Do what you will with us. Fulfill your fantasies."

He fought to urge to pinch himself. This was no dream. Once again, he would get to make love to two beautiful women ... only, this time, he would not miss the chance he had foregone many times before. This last time they had her, he would take Petra in the ways he'd been fantasizing about since the moment he'd met her.

Coming toward them, he reached out and grasped the nape of Petra's neck. Lowering his head, he kissed her, sweeping the inside of her mouth with his tongue. Pressing his body to hers, he felt Cecily's hand between them, working Petra's cunt.

Tearing his lips away from hers, he lowered them to her breasts. Teasing each nipple with his open mouth, he flicked his tongue over the peaks, then took them both between his teeth one at a time with playful nips. She moaned, arching her back and leaning more heavily on Cecily, who continued nibbling on her neck and fingering her beneath the nightgown.

Reaching down, he grasped her hips and lifted her, wrapping her legs around his waist. She held onto his neck and gazed down at him through eyes gone dark and limpid from desire. Her gown had come up to her waist, giving him access to her wet cunt. Cecily's ministrations had her dripping with desire and ready for him. But there remained so much more he wanted to do to her first—to them both.

Moving his hips, he brushed the head of his cock against the opening of her core, but held back from entering her. Her juices drenched him, and they both emitted low moans at the contact. Grasping the cheeks of her buttocks, he ground her against him, rubbing his thick shaft between her lower lips and caressing her swollen clitoris.

Walking over to the bed, he deposited her on top of the counterpane. Turning, he found Cecily waiting for him. He pulled her against him, molding her body against his. She was so different from the woman awaiting them on the bed—fuller, plumper, buxom. Reaching up to the neckline of her gown, he gripped the lace and pulled, tearing it down the middle. He chuckled at her sharp gasp.

"That was expensive!" she exclaimed.

He shrugged, peeling the fabric away and letting it pool at her feet. "I'll buy a hundred more of the blasted things, so long as I get to be the one to rip them off."

She giggled as he lifted her, too, and deposited her upon the bed beside Petra. "Anything you want, my lord."

Her words sent a fresh surge of blood to his already straining cock.

Anything he wanted.

They were both his for the taking; yet, he hardly knew where to begin.

Glancing down at the two pairs of lovely breasts spread before him like offerings on a buffet, he decided to begin there.

Crawling up onto the bed, placing one knee between each of their spread legs, he bent over them. Catching one of Cecily's nipples between his lips, he suckled hungrily. Reaching toward Petra, he palmed one of her breasts, twisting the nipple between his thumb and forefinger.

Cecily moaned, arching her back as Petra slid a hand between her legs. He continued suckling her breasts, moving back and forth from one to the other, while Petra parted Cecily's lips and inner folds to reveal the moist, pink center of her cunt. Cecily moaned and thrashed as he teased her nipples and Petra tickled her clit.

Moving his hand down from her breast, he found his way between

Petra's legs. She spread them wider for him, inviting him in. His thumb circled her clit, while his forefinger dipped inside her tight, velvety channel. Both women trembled, writhing beneath him. He moved his lips from Cecily to Petra, reveling in the feel of her nipples against his tongue and the feel of her around his fingers.

"You like my wife's sweet cunt, don't you?" he asked her, stilling his fingers inside of her.

She strained toward him, bucking her hips and taking him back inside of her. "Yes," she replied, her voice husky with desire.

He smiled, obliging her with a few more strokes inside her channel, coating his digits with more of her honey.

"Cecily, darling, I want you to straddle Petra's face and let her taste your sweet quim." Removing his fingers, he brought them to his fingers and tasted them. "Hmmm," he moaned. "I must have more."

Lowering his head between Petra's legs, he glanced up, watching as Cecily climbed up and spread her legs, lowering her cunt toward Petra's face. He reached down and stroked himself, driven wild with lust at the sight of Petra's pink tongue lapping at his wife's cunt.

Cecily moaned, resting on her hands and knees while Petra licked and suckled her clitoris, her hands palming the cheeks of her buttocks and kneading them.

Spreading the lips of Petra's core, he revealed her tender pink flesh dripping with arousal. His tongue tingled when he pressed it against her. Lapping and suckling, he eased his hunger by filling his mouth with her taste. Her moans were muffled as she continued performing the same act on Cecily, joining her lips and tongue with her fingers. Spreading her legs wider, he did the same, thrusting two fingers into her slick channel and pumping them in and out while sucking her clitoris.

With his opposite hand, he pumped his erection, easing the ache caused by the taste of Petra and the sight of Cecily riding the other woman's tongue, her hips thrusting as she threw her head back and played with her erect nipples.

He wanted more now. His own ministrations were no longer

enough to soothe him with so much tantalizing, feminine flesh just within his grasp.

Kneeling between Petra's spread legs, he positioned himself to enter her. Reaching for Cecily, he pulled her down between them, resting her on top of Petra. Running his fingers down her spine, he leaned down to kiss the back of her neck.

Arching her back, she ground her hips against Petra's and moaned. The woman's answering sound proved the last straw.

Unable to hold back any longer, he slammed into Petra, entering her in one forceful stroke. She screamed, arching her back as he pulled back and entered again, finding a steady rhythm.

Reaching down between Cecily's legs, he encountered Petra's fingers. The Madame had already reached back, hooking one of Cecily's legs upward, sliding her arm between their bodies, and begun thrusting her slender digits in and out of his wife's cunt. Cecily bent her head toward Petra's and the two kissed, tongues dueling as his cock pounded in and out of Petra, and her fingers slid in and out of Cecily.

Glancing down at the beautiful, round backside bouncing against his abdomen, he was struck with the urge to explore his wife in a way he never had before. Without hesitating to question whether it might be proper, he spread her buttocks, revealing her tight anus. Reaching down to coat his fingers in the honey that Petra had coaxed from her cunt, he smeared up over the forbidden passage. Pressing his finger against it, he grinned as she shivered and moaned. The high-pitched sound indicated her surprise and pleasure.

"Do you like that, sweetheart?" he whispered, sinking his finger in inch by slow inch. Below him, Petra continued thrusting into her channel with insistent fingers, while lower still, his cock moved in and out of Petra's silken sheath.

She whimpered, wiggling her hips and angling her bottom higher so that he could continue his invasion. Beneath her, Petra suckled and fondled Cecily's breasts while lifting her hips to meet Sheridan's.

He watched in fascination as his finger sank deeper and deeper into her back passage, squeezed tight by the virginal, unexplored ring of flesh. She trembled and moaned as he slid his finger slowly in and out, imagining that tight channel wrapped around his cock. Just the thought nearly drove him over the edge, and he quickened his strokes within Petra, satisfied by the hitch in her breath as her thighs clenched around his.

Cecily shattered first, screaming out her release and pressing her hips back against the hands teasing her to completion. Sheridan moved faster inside her back passage, heightening her pleasure. She screamed, throwing her head back and trembling, before collapsing on top of Petra, who shattered second. She wrapped her arms around Cecily, capturing her lips and moaning as Sheridan grasped her thighs and lifted, angling her for deeper penetration.

He gasped as her sheath tightened around him, pulsating in release. He bit his lower lip, fighting not to come just yet, waiting until just the right moment. Holding on as long as he could, he gritted his teeth and continued stroking inside of her, his legs trembling as the inevitable climax nipped at his heels. It nearly crippled him, causing his bollocks to contract and forcing the air from his lungs. He felt certain his tight grip left fingerprints on Petra's thighs as he dug into them and lunged one last time.

Pulling away slowly, he collapsed on the bed beside Cecily, who had rolled from on top of Petra to lie between them. Pulling her against him, he kissed her temple, then her cheek. Smiling, she turned her head and kissed him back.

Relief swept through him. While he'd known having Petra with them was something his wife had desired, he'd also worried that she would find watching him have sex with another woman to be distasteful, after all.

However, his wife had been sated and seemed pleased as she lay sandwiched between her two lovers. Draping one arm over Petra, who lay nestled against her, she closed her eyes.

Reaching down, he found the counterpane and pulled it over the three of them. As his racing breath began to calm, he held his wife and began drifting off toward sleep.

Cecily opened her eyes and smiled. The morning sun filtered through the windows, slightly stinging her eyes. Stretching, she came to full wakefulness, reliving every moment of the night before with a grin. A slow throb began between her thighs as the memories awakened her with insistent longing. Turning onto her side, she frowned to find the bed empty where Petra had once laid.

Lifting herself up onto her elbow, she scanned the room, finding it cleared of Petra's belongings. She'd brought a valise that had gone missing, and the discarded nightgown was gone, as well. Sitting up fully, she glanced over at Sheridan, who still lay sleeping on his stomach beside her. Rising from the bed, she located her robe and slipped it on. Walking toward her dressing room, she listened for any sound that might indicate the woman might be on the other side of the door.

Instead of Petra, she found a crisp, white envelope resting on her washstand. Their names had been scrawled on it in a neat hand.

Cecily and Sheridan.

Curiosity gnawing on her insides, she opened the envelope and found a thick sheet of stationary inside. She recognized it from the writing desk in her room. Trudging back into the bedroom, she read the note.

Dear Cecily and Sheridan,

I thought to leave before your servants intruded. Imagine the shock if they were to find me in your bed!

Last night was quite an experience, and I thoroughly enjoyed every moment of it. Thank you for inviting me into your lives, your marriage, and your bed. I am thrilled to see the progress that you have made as a couple. Nothing brings me more joy than helping people explore each other in new ways.

Do call on me if you ever find yourselves wanting to invite another woman into your bed. I, or one of my girls, would be more than happy to oblige you.

Yours sincerely,

Petra

On the bed, Sheridan rolled over and stretched with a groan.

She perched on the mattress beside him and waited for him to come fully awake. He brushed the hair out of his eyes and peered up at her. A slow smile creased his face covered by a night's worth of stubble.

"Good morning, love. Where's Petra?"

Holding up the note where he could see it, she shrugged. "Gone. She wanted to leave before the servants could discover her."

He chuckled, the sound much deeper with the clinging talons of sleep in his voice. Cecily quite liked it.

"Could you imagine their horror if they had? As if we haven't caused enough scandal."

She slid back into bed beside him, allowing him to nestle the coverlet around her.

"I do believe I am the one who started the last one. I will thank you not to take all the credit."

Sheridan's hand slipped beneath her dressing gown and he fondled her buttocks.

"Hmm, my naughty little wife. Whatever shall I do with you?"

She lay back and let him untie the belt of her robe, sighing when his hands found her bare flesh.

"Whatever you wish, my love," she replied. "I am yours to do with as you please."

He nuzzled her neck, the stubble along his jaw tickling her. "That leaves us open to so many delicious possibilities," he mumbled, nibbling at her shoulder. "It sounds like the makings of quite a marriage."

"A passionate marriage," she replied, arching her back as his tongue caressed one of her nipples. Then, thinking of Petra, she giggled. "No, a scandalous one."

He glanced up and their gazes met, and she knew he thought of Petra, too. Perhaps someday, they would invite her into their bed again, or someone else. Cecily found she'd enjoyed sharing her husband with another woman. However, for now, she felt content to be with him, reveling in their love and the little life she would bring into the world the following summer.

"A marriage most scandalous," he repeated, nodding. "Yes, I quite like the sound of that."

ABOUT THE AUTHOR

Sexy heroes ... sassy heroines ... electrifying erotic romance.
Victoria Vale has written over two dozen Romance and Young Adult
novels under various pseudonyms. As a lover of erotic romance, she
enjoys nothing more than a sexy hero paired with a sassy heroine,
flavored with a dash of spice and lots of heat. A wife and mother of
three, she enjoys reading (of course), cooking, sewing ... and other
activities that aren't appropriate for inclusion in a biography.

www.ingramcontent.com/pod-product-compliance
Lightning Source LLC
Chambersburg PA
CBHW030331160726
47992CB00005B/2244